What Pe

"What happens when three children walk into a magical closet and end up in Puerto Rico? Author, María Pérez-Gómez, cleverly weaves Puerto Rican culture, history, and folklore into a story with unexpected turns and twists as the children, now in animal form, work to help their beloved homeland regain hope after two devastating hurricanes. As with any life adventure, real or imaginary, what they learn about love, loss, and hope permeates every step. It is a cultural contribution to the genre of children's literature that I recommend to school libraries and classroom teachers."

—Janyne McConnaughey, PhD, Trauma-Informed Author & Advocate, Author of Trauma in the Pews

"*The Magical Closet Mystery* by María Pérez-Gómez is a celebration of childhood imagination in the context of Puerto Rican culture. The children are having difficulty coping with the loss of their father and a move from Puerto Rico to Buffalo, NY. Suddenly, they are transformed into animals and transported to Puerto Rico, through their bedroom closet, by the magic of Puerto Rico. The resulting adventure is both entertaining and educational, and illustrates the healing power of art, music, and cultural heritage. Bravo!"

—Michael A. Cline, NP

"Bravo! A masterfully written story that weaves together the robust culture and history of Puerto Rico while acknowledging the struggle of moving to a new land and finding hope in the midst of grief. María uses tactful and descriptive language to spark imagination and produce powerful emotions while evoking a new appreciation for the food, art, music, and beauty of Puerto Rican culture. This timeless message entwines themes such as courage, empathy, love, suffering, and hope in a single story that will leave children and adults alike with a renewed sense of purpose. *The Magical Closet Mystery* will surely become a household staple for many, a story that brings new meaning every time it's read."

—Abigail J. Grainge, MS, FNP

"María has combined her love for Puerto Rico with deep and comforting wisdom. Luca's search is a beautiful journey that can and should be shared by everyone, children and adults alike."

—Kyle LoConti, Professor Emeritus of Theatre Arts,
Theater Educator and Director

"*The Magical Closet Mystery* is a beautiful, modern-day parable filled with heart, humor, laughter, and love. After reading just the first few paragraphs, the characters come to life and lead you on an adventure where you learn that whatever you hold most dear and keep close to your heart can never truly be lost."

—John Anderson,
Kenmore Presbyterian Church Elder/Father

"This book is an enchanting and magical story, told through the lens of Puerto Rican culture but readily appreciated by those of any cultural background. Aside from weaving a beautiful tale of family, friendship, and community, *The Magical Closet Mystery* seeks to help children who may be dealing with trauma find hope and understanding. It points to the importance of expressing feelings and connecting to positive aspects of the character's lives and their personal and cultural histories. Ms. Pérez-Gómez communicates these messages through the story of three young Puerto Rican children, now living in Buffalo, who are mourning the death of their father, the loss of their homeland, and the devastation of the hurricanes that swept through their beloved Puerto Rico. Their lives are changed completely when they discover a portal in their bedroom closet that leads to wild adventure, tender awakening, and individual and communal healing in the lush Puerto Rican rainforest. Ms. Pérez-Gómez's beautifully descriptive writing style transports the reader to the delightful sights, sounds, and fragrant scents of Puerto Rico, but her message of courage, connection, and healing is as universal as the transcendent power of love itself."

—Roberta Farkas-Huezo, MSW, Child Welfare Administrator, Erie County Department of Social Services

"*The Magical Closet Mystery* is the lost love letter that needs to be found and read by our people, our island's descendants, and the world! I always carry internal pride when it comes to my Puerto Rican identity. But this book's words were a reawakening of love and pride as I was reminded of our island's beautiful, magical existence and its people. As I journeyed with the main characters, I was touched by the lessons of love, loss, and resilience. I was pleasantly surprised by its depth, wisdom, and mysticism. Our traditions and culture are exposed so richly as we realize that we are the vessels on which they continue to live. *The Magical Closet Mystery* is a must read for children and adults alike."

—Jeanette Torres, Advanced Medical Support Assistant at the US Department of Veterans Affairs in Buffalo, NY

"Enchanting, engaging, and educational! *The Magical Closet Mystery* is a beautiful well-researched story that will no doubt be loved by children and adults alike. Magia, Luca, and Mateo, the story's main characters, guide you through a magical journey where they meet memorable friends that teach them about healing, music, friendship, and the magic that lives in each of us. This is the perfect book to give a child dealing with grief and homesickness. The author weaves the story in a way that allows the child to expand their imagination while learning about the culture and history of Puerto Rico. I recommend this book to teachers looking for new material for their pupils and anyone who wants to go on a magic ride. It was a pleasure to read."

—Ingrid Córdova, Actor

"*The Magical Closet Mystery* is a story that allows accessibility to another culture and language in a way that is magical, fun, and entertaining. Every one of us has a unique voice and has something to offer others that speaks of hope, love, unity, forgiveness, healing, and acceptance."

—Jennifer Anderson,
Teacher Assistant in Special Education

"Imaginative, informative, and a whole lot of fun, the reader (whether parent or child) and listener can hear the voices and music, smell the air and food, and see the worlds shape and shift before their eyes. This evocative book will transport young and old alike, reminding them that even the most magical journey doesn't take the place of home."

—Kate LoConti Alcocer, Executive Artistic Director of Irish Classical Theatre Company

"*The Magical Closet Mystery* is a love song to Puerto Rico. The writer's love for music and her island shines through every page. Combining humor, emotional intelligence, and the importance of remembering where you came from, this book captivates and speaks to the hearts of readers from every generation. Given the grief we are all experiencing as a whole, this book will pluck your heartstrings and give you hope for a better tomorrow."

—Sara Rodríguez, Artist

"María Pérez-Gómez has added 'author' to her repertoire! *The Magical Closet Mystery* is a gorgeous story of young siblings that lovingly weave heritage and healing into the music of magic."

—Matthew Tice, LCSW,
Director of VIVE Refugee Shelter

"*The Magical Closet Mystery* is one of those books that is so embedded with the pain, and ultimately, hope of its main characters that you can't help but empathize from the first sentence. María is a gifted writer who has magically allowed for the transference of her love of Puerto Rico, her understanding of living in the diaspora, and her emotional intelligence demonstrated in her compassion during grief to be translated into a book for children. This book has truly overwhelmingly deepened my love for storytelling. The magic she was able to ignite through the eyes of these characters is the stuff dreams are made of. Bravo!"

—Victoria Pérez, Artistic Director, Actor

A PUERTO RICAN ADVENTURE

the Magical Closet Mystery

María Pérez-Gómez

Illustrated by Carlos Torres

The Magical Closet Mystery: A Puerto Rican Adventure

First paperback edition October 2022
Cover art and illustrations by Carlos Torres
Published by Berry Powell Press
Glendora, CA

ISBN: 978-1-957321-08-0 (Paperback)
ISBN: 978-1-957321-09-7 (ebook)

Library of Congress Control Number: 2022918276

Dedication

"Puerto Rico tierra grata que con pena te dejé."
Rafael Pérez

Translation:
"Puerto Rico, beloved homeland,
with sorrow I left thee."

My love letter to Puerto Rico
In honor of my father, Rafael Pérez
In memory of my brother, Oscar Roberto Pérez

CONTENTS

CHAPTER 1

"Why do you have to leave? Why can't *Abuela* find someone else to help her!" Luca complained as *Mami* packed. He was tall for a ten-year-old and athletic from years of baseball. But right now, with his pleading brown puppy dog eyes, he looked like a child half his age. He stormed out of the living room and up the stairs toward his bedroom, making sure he marked every creaky wooden step with a loud stomp.

Abuela: Grandmother

Mami: Mother; Mommy; Mom

Reaching the bedroom Luca shared with his little brother, Mateo, he jumped onto his bed and threw his comforter over his head. The comforter was bright red matching his cheeks, which became rosy even through his dark complexion.

Mami followed him into his room, just as he had hoped she would. The bed shifted as she sat down by the lump where his knees were. Her long, dark hair fell forward, sweeping the comforter as she leaned toward her son. Her deep almond eyes glistened with concern.

"*Ay* Luca, aren't you glad your grandmother will live with us soon?" Every word spoken by Mami was candy-coated with deep love and kindness, making Luca feel almost guilty. Almost.

ay: oh

"Yes, I am!" His voice came out muffled by the comforter. And it was true. Luca couldn't wait for Abuela to get here so they could make his favorite dessert, *arroz con dulce.* They'd devour the sweet, coconutty cinnamon rice all on their own during the domino tournaments they always had when she visited. "But why can't she just fly here on her own? She's a grownup, not a kid like me."

arroz con dulce: Puerto Rican rice pudding

Mami caressed Luca's coiled black hair through the comforter. "You know that your abuela needs more help now that she's older. This is what Puerto Ricans do—we take care of our people when they get older."

"Okay, then. Why can't *Tía* go instead?"

Tía: Aunt; Auntie

"You know how much Tía Clara hates flying. Besides, she's going to stay here and watch you three."

Mami continued to quietly pat Luca's head through the comforter, which irritated Luca even more. He squirmed a little further.

"I don't want Tía Clara to stay here! I want you to stay. But *noooo*! You *have* to go!" he said. "This stinks!"

Luca felt a shift in his chest as his fierce anger faded to a more sad and hollow feeling.

"Mami, can't we think of another solution? There is always more than one solution to a problem. *Papi* always said that." Luca's tone softened as he mentioned his father. He knew he was wrong to bring Papi into this, but he was desperate.

Papi: Father; Dad; Daddy

If he had said this six months ago, Mami might have given in. Now, she remained quiet for several moments, tapping her finger on Luca's pillow. Still hidden under the comforter, Luca could imagine the deep crease forming between Mami's eyebrows that appeared when she was thinking hard. Taking a deep breath, she stood up.

Mami responded softly but firmly. "I'm sorry you are upset, Luca. But I'm going to California to get Abuela packed, and I'll bring her back before you know it."

"No, you won't!" He finally pulled the covers off his head. "Two weeks equals fourteen days, and fourteen days is a really long time!"

Mami kissed his forehead. A car's horn blared out front.

"The taxi's here!" Luca's older sister, Magia, called upstairs from the front door below.

"I have to go now, *mi amor*," Mami said to Luca.

mi amor:
my love

He yanked the comforter back over his head, refusing to say goodbye.

Mami let out a deep sigh, then walked into the hall toward the door where her two other children and Tía Clara were standing by her luggage. Tía Clara's eyes met Mami's with knowing compassion.

Tía wiped her strong hands on her floral apron and pulled her thick, gray-streaked hair into a low bun like she was ready for anything. She grasped Mami's hand and whispered into her ear, "Don't worry. I will take good care of your babies."

Mami smiled and kissed her aunt's soft cheek. "I know, Tía. It means so much to me that you're here with them."

She reached down to kiss Magia on the cheek too. Magia beamed back up at her, fierce and dutiful, with her wild dark wavy hair wrapped into two long braids. At twelve, Magia was the oldest, never mind that eight-year-old Mateo was almost outgrowing her in height. But physical size meant nothing to this child.

"Don't worry, Mami. I'll make sure the boys stay in line."

"Thank you. I know you will." Mami chuckled. "Oh, please make sure Mateo eats at least one vegetable this week. You know where the phone numbers are in case something—"

"We'll be *fine*, Mami!"

"I know. Just..." Mami quieted her voice and flickered her eyes toward the upstairs. "Will you check on him?"

Magia nodded dutifully. Mami's deep brown eyes crinkled as she smiled at her daughter. "I know I can always count on you." Turning to Mateo, Mami kissed his cheek and then looked into his blue eyes. "I will be back so soon, *mi amor*. I will call every day!" Mateo stood on his tippy-toes and kissed her back.

"I know, Mami. Bring us back something cool!" His cheeks rounded as he flashed her a cheesy smile. She swept his sandy blonde hair away from his eyes.

Mami picked up her luggage and walked past their little vegetable garden in the yard to the taxi at the curb. A man in dark blue got out and loaded her bags into the car.

Mateo hollered, "Luca! Mami is leaving. It's your last chance to say goodbye!" There was no response. Mateo said, "Maybe it makes him too sad to watch?"

Mateo's eight-year-old wisdom matched the famous Puerto Rican saying, "Eyes that don't see, a heart that doesn't feel,"—the English equivalent, "Out of sight, out of mind!"

"Maybe." Magia shrugged her shoulders.

Mami got in, and the cab driver closed the door. "I miss you already!" Mami called from the taxi. Magia and Mateo watched Mami go, with Tía standing behind them. Their bubbliness faded as they watched the car door close, and a quiet sadness filled the air. They all knew it was important for Mami to help Abuela Nivian, but no one liked to see Mami go.

"I wish Luca had come down," Mateo broke the silence.

"Me too." Magia put her arm around her little brother, pretending to comfort him, but she was the one who had secret tears forming in her eyes. The three stood in the doorway and waved goodbye as the taxi disappeared down the street.

Family had been the most important thing, as far back as the kids could remember. They were nearly inseparable from one another—even more so since they moved to Buffalo. Everything was new, strange, and so different from Puerto Rico. They stuck together in school—or they had, until other kids began calling Magia their "bodyguard." Luca got embarrassed, especially since he was the self-assigned man of the family, so much taller than Magia, and now the shortstop on his baseball team. Still, they'd spent almost every evening together, playing games on the floor, doing homework, or huddled around the TV with dinner. Being with one another was the only thing that remained consistent when they moved from Puerto Rico to Buffalo, New York, last year.

Puerto Rico and Buffalo could not be more different. Puerto Rico was in the Caribbean and had one season all year long: summer. Buffalo had four seasons: spring, summer, fall, and winter. Most of the time felt like winter. The kids couldn't get used to all the layers needed to keep warm: a coat, mittens, a hat, boots, and a scarf! The family heard Mateo complaining every morning before school, "Mami, I can't even move! I've got pants under my pants! I feel like a mummy!" Mami would then make him "mummy walk" out the door, taking tiny, stiff steps with his arms straight in front of him.

Oh, how they missed the delicious tropical fruit that colorfully dotted the path on their way to school. They ate guava, passionfruit, and mangos right off the trees as they walked by. Although Buffalo did have red, orange, and yellow leaves in the fall, they still lacked tropical fruit. Missing, too, were the sounds of Puerto Rico: the echoing rooster crow each morning and the soothing bedtime lullaby of the croaking *coquí.* The kids could hardly fall asleep at first without the rhythmic song of that little brown frog, which, to them and their people, symbolized Puerto Rico itself.

coquí: a miniature tree frog known as the national symbol of Puerto Rico.

It had been hard for the children to make friends when they first moved to New York State. They repeatedly heard the question, "Why do you all look so different if you're from the same family?"

It was true; they did look different. Why was Mateo the only one with blue eyes, and why did only Luca have curly hair?

One morning at breakfast, Luca asked Mami, "Why don't we all look the same?"

Mami smiled wide. "Puerto Ricans are like the surprise in a Cracker Jack box; you never know what you're gonna get! Taino, African, or European features—or a mixture of all three!" she answered.

Testing out this new information, the kids evaluated each family member. Mami had features of the Taino people who were indigenous to Puerto Rico. She was smaller in stature and had a dark golden tone to her skin with long, straight, jet-black hair. But their Papi was quite tall with lighter caramel skin from European ancestors and the tight black curls of the enslaved Africans brought from Africa to Puerto Rico.

Magia took after her mother in size, but her hair was more European with loose brown waves. Luca was tall with tight curly hair like Papi but with Mami's almond-shaped eyes. Mateo had light brownish-blonde hair with European eyes, the color of Puerto Rico's blue ocean. No wonder people had difficulty believing they were in the same family!

Once the door was closed, Tía Clara bent down and hugged the two kids. The house felt emptier with Mami gone and Luca refusing to come down. To distract everyone from the sadness, Tía stood up, put on a happy face, and made an announcement into an imaginary microphone.

"Ladies and gentlemen, the moment you've all been waiting for!" Eyeing Mateo and Magia, she winked playfully and continued. "It's pizza *pastelillo* time!"

"Yes!" Mateo clapped his hands.

"*Delicioso*!" Magia said. She smiled as Tía headed for the kitchen while shaking her hips and dancing to an imaginary salsa song.

They were ready to follow her into the kitchen for tasty pizza turnovers when they heard a loud blast that sounded like a cross between a foghorn and a dying elephant. They stopped in their tracks. Mateo looked up at his sister. "Magia, what was *that*?"

pastelillo: Puerto Rican turnover pastry

delicioso: delicious

CHAPTER 2

"It's coming from your room," Magia whispered. She was referring to the bedroom that her brothers shared. Magia had her own room. "One of the perks of being the only girl," she would often say.

"Do you think Luca is attempting to play his trumpet?" Magia asked, looking up at her brother.

Mateo wrinkled his face as if biting into a sour lemon. "I have never heard him get that sound out of his trumpet. Maybe he's got a wild animal in there!"

"Mateo, I think something is very wrong with him!" Magia admitted. "It sounds terrible and sad and… well, terrible!"

"Let's go stop him…I mean help him…before we go deaf!" Mateo said. His brows were furrowed, and he had his hands over his ears.

They marched up the stairs in synchronized, rhythmic steps, taking each step with purpose and determination. They flung open the door to the bedroom, expecting to see Luca sitting on his bed, practicing his trumpet. Instead, they saw a large lump of something under the red comforter. The heap rocked from side to side and emitted sounds that could only be coming from something or someone in pain. With grave concern, Magia and Mateo slowly approached his bed, ready to save Luca's life from the awful creature that had wiped all musical ability from his memory. "One, two, three," they silently mouthed, and ripped away the blanket.

Luca was crumpled into a ball. His grimacing face and puffy red eyes were now exposed as if he were a wild animal. He snatched the blanket and pulled it back over his head. Magia and Mateo looked at each other.

"Stop this right now!" Magia was taking charge as usual. "You can't play the trumpet under a blanket."

"Oh, yes I can!" Luca bellowed stubbornly. "I can, and I am!"

Mateo put his hand on Magia's arm and whispered, "Let me try." He sat on the corner of the bed and tried a different tactic. "Luca?" Mateo asked gently.

"What?" Luca shot back.

"Will you come out and talk to me?"

"No!"

"Please? Are you crying?"

"No!"

"Then why are you hiding?"

Luca sighed dramatically and slowly pulled the blanket down just below his eyes. "I'm not hiding. I'm practicing my trumpet in privacy. Plus, I don't have to answer to you. You're not the boss around here, okay? While Mami's gone, you should be listening to *me!*"

Magia rolled her eyes. "Look, if anyone is in charge, it's me! I'm the oldest."

Luca folded his arms in defiance. "But I'm the oldest boy! That makes *me* the man of the house." This was a role he'd assigned himself sometime in the last several months. Maybe he heard it on one of his television shows. No one quite knew where he got the idea. Magia rolled her eyes, incredibly irritated now that Luca thought he could replace their Papi.

Their Papi died a year and a half earlier when they lived in Puerto Rico. It was so sudden. Sure, they knew it was dangerous putting out fires for a living. While it was something they always feared, it was never something they felt could become their reality. One day, the Fire Chief came to their house and told them that Papi had bravely entered a burning house just before it collapsed. He rescued three people but inhaled too much smoke in the process. He was never coming home again.

The months following were either very loud or very quiet. Sometimes it was weeping, yelling, laughing at old memories, and accepting food from neighbors. Other times, it was utterly silent, the home filled with an emptiness no words could soothe.

One night during dinner, Mami said, "It is so hard living in this house with all of our memories."

Magia agreed. "I keep thinking Papi will walk in the door as if nothing happened."

Mateo whispered, "But he never does."

Luca sat stone-faced, saying nothing. He wished everyone would stop talking about Papi because it always made him feel so sad. He tried to think of anything other than how much he missed Papi.

This tragedy was Luca's most painful experience in his young life. Memories were in every corner of their home. The photos on the wall of Papi in uniform reminded them of what had taken him away. Papi had been brave. Now he was *gone*. Gone were the chances to be picked up from school on Papi's days off. Gone was the laughter they shared when he would take them to buy *piraguas* at the corner store. Gone were the bedtime stories and the songs. Gone was the strumming of his *cuatro* and the music filling their home. Gone were the Mami and Papi dances in the living room and silly dance moves with Magia, Luca, and Mateo. All of it was gone. It was too painful to think about, let alone talk about it.

piragua: a beloved Puerto Rican dessert made of shaved ice and fruit-flavored syrup.

cuatro: Puerto Rico's national instrument. It's smaller than a guitar, but larger than a mandolin, and it has five double strings

One Sunday afternoon, when they were sitting around watching television and feeling especially sad, Mami walked into the room to share an important decision she had made. "We need a fresh start, and we have an aunt who lives in Buffalo, Tía Clara."

Mateo asked, "How does Tía Clara live inside a buffalo?"

Luca poked him with his elbow. "No, silly. Buffalo is a city in New York, in the United States."

Mami nodded. "Yes, we need to start fresh there." It was the reason she gave for leaving their beloved little home—their *casita*—in Puerto Rico. "A fresh start." She said it over and over as they packed, as if she were studying for a big test and she needed to remember the correct answer to pass when the time came.

casita: little house, or little home

So, they moved to Buffalo. Only now, it felt worse to Luca because along with missing his Papi, he missed Puerto Rico too! *Moving was a bad plan.* He had tried to make friends but still felt like an outsider. He started taking trumpet lessons, and that was a little help. It felt like he was blowing out his sadness. But most of all, he just wanted to pretend it never happened. It was easier to do when they were all together. When Mami left, it was more challenging.

Even though Luca wouldn't admit it to a single soul, he always got upset when Mami went away. Mami often had to go away for a weekend business trip. She ensured they were safe and well taken care of by her Tía Clara, but even Magia agreed that it wasn't the same when Mami was gone. Luca sulked with a sad, sour look on his face. If anyone asked him if he was upset, he'd shake his head "no."

Magia whispered in Mateo's ear, "If we don't help him snap out of it, he may sulk the entire time Mami is gone."

As if on cue, Luca pulled the bedspread over his head again and put his lips to his trumpet. The room shook with the ghastliest ear-splitting sound he could blow. "Worse yet, he could play that horrible song the entire time Mami is gone!" Mateo yelled back over the loud wail.

They nodded to each other in agreement. Magia and Mateo had to do something to help Luca feel better. Magia believed she knew exactly what that was: tell her brothers a story. When Mami wasn't around, and it was just the three of them, Magia made up stories about Puerto Rico. Being the oldest, she remembered and understood the most about their beloved island. Some stories were based on real things that had happened. Still, lately, Magia had created more stories filled with magic and mythical creatures from Puerto Rican folklore. Mateo loved to hear these stories. In spite of himself, Luca also felt better after Magia told them a tall tale of how perfect life would be if they could just move back, because Magia's stories always had a happy ending. If only they could return to Puerto Rico, everything would be perfect.

Magia leaped into action like a performer who had just received her cue. She got up on a chair and shouted, "Let me have your attention, *por favor*!"

por favor: please

This was how her stories always started, with a big declaration, to get her brothers to settle into their seats and quiet their cellphones. Luca stopped playing and sat up against his headboard. Mateo crawled onto Luca's bed, relieved for the quiet as all trumpet sounds subsided. None of them could resist a good story. Stories were the glue of their family—stories of adventure and family and their people. Mateo sat next to Luca who put a pillow on his lap. Luca didn't seem excited for the story, but he didn't stop her either.

"I have a story for you! The setting, Puerto Rico!"

CHAPTER 3

"Once upon a time, there were two brothers and a sister. The oldest of the three was a girl. She loved nature, her brothers, and Puerto Rico. The middle child loved playing the trumpet, playing on the baseball diamond, and Puerto Rico. The youngest loved food, telling jokes, and—yes, you guessed it—Puerto Rico. Puerto Rico had been their home always until a year and a half ago."

Luca had a scowl on his face, so she knew that this story had to be the best one she'd ever told to keep him from playing the trumpet. She went on. "All three of them missed the sun, the warm breeze, and eating mango from the trees on their way to school. They especially missed the days when the baker would drive down the street announcing, 'There's bread! Fresh bread! Cornbread and *dulces*!' Close your eyes and remember the street sounds. Can you hear the coquís, the roosters, and pigs? Can you feel the breeze? Can you," she paused to build excitement as she squealed with delight, "smell the fresh bread? Oh! Puerto Rico is so magical."

dulces: desserts or candy

Mateo, playing along, closed his eyes and held his hands close to his face; cupping his nose, he took a deep breath. "Oh, yes!"

Luca just shook his head, the comforter rustling around him. "This story is dumb."

Magia had been hopeful that the memories of the island would be enough to transport both of her brothers, especially Luca, into a whole new world. In this world, he would forget. But he seemed to be even grumpier. *How can I turn this around?* An idea sprung into her mind.

"Until one day, the three discovered a magical entrance. A secret doorway between two worlds that no one else had ever found before. Where was this magical doorway, you ask?" Mateo leaned in. Luca looked mildly interested.

"Well, like most magical doorways, it was able to hide in a place you'd least expect it to be—in plain sight!" She snapped the last word with suspense and the boys jumped. She pointed over to the boys' closet, a dark wooden door with a weathered, brass knob. "A door just like that!"

Luca rolled his eyes. "Our closet? This story is boring." He put the pillow over his face.

Magia didn't allow Luca to ruffle her. She leaned back with a cool, controlled nonchalance. "But in order for the doorway to be opened, it needed to be activated by something."

"What does 'activated' mean?" Mateo looked over at Luca.

From under the comforter, he said, "It means it needs something to turn it on for it to work."

Luca pulled the cover from his head, ready to challenge his sister. "Well, Magia. What activates it? How did they get back to Puerto Rico?" He pressed her impatiently.

"Well, that's an excellent que—" Magia stalled while she thought of an answer, but she trailed off at the faint sound of music.

The boys' eyes scanned the room, and their ears perked up.

"Did you hear that?" Mateo asked.

Magia said, "I hear singing."

"Magia, are you doing that? Did you hide your speaker in my closet?" Luca groaned at his sister, trying to hide his curiosity. This was certainly an elaborate scheme if she did, and he was almost impressed.

"No, I swear I'm not." She began defending herself, but then remembered she was the storyteller. She might as well take credit for it. She snapped back into character. "I swear I'm not making this up. Yes, it's all part of the story, boys. You underestimate how good I am."

Faint as it was, they'd recognize those words anywhere, anytime, and it was unmistakably the very sound of Puerto Rico.

"It's the *Le Lo Lai*!" Mateo declared.

It was a phrase that could be put to any music, woven into any song. It reminded Puerto Ricans of their wonderful homeland, no matter where they were. It was like a secret message that Puerto Ricans shared. The children were stunned to hear these words drifting across the room in a beautiful melody.

Le Lo Lai: a phrase often used in poetry or song reminding Puerto Ricans of their beloved island

"And it's coming out of the closet!" Luca observed, leaning forward. "Come on, Magia. How are you doing this?"

Scan this code to listen to the Magical Closet song.

Magia didn't answer. Truthfully, she was a little startled. *Where is this song coming from?*

"I hope your speaker is buried under my last week's game uniform. You're going to be the one to get it! Ninety degrees that day, so it's going to be nice and stinky with my manly stench!"

"You should have put it straight into the washer, like Mami told you to!" Magia winced, horrified.

"Nope. I like letting it marinate, like *pernil* sitting in its juices before going into the oven

pernil: Marinated pork shoulder with crispy skin.

the morning of Christmas." At this, he finally cracked a smile. He was enjoying this too much.

Mateo piped up. "Maybe the song is what activates it!"

"Oh, something in there is *activated* all right." Luca smirked at Magia. "Let's go smell…I mean, see."

Three pairs of children's feet landed on the shaggy floor and padded over to the closet. Mateo clung to his sister's hand as Luca reached for the shiny doorknob, eager to expose Magia's Bluetooth speaker beneath his smelly clothes. But as they moved closer to the door, even he sensed as if something strange was happening. The doorknob was warm—hot. And as he touched it, a light glow surrounded them.

The instant the door cracked open, a flash of white light filled the room and the sound of crackling thunder roared in their ears. A mighty wind sucked them in toward the closet. Startled and confused, they all screamed and grabbed each other's hands. They tried to resist the wind and turn back into the bedroom, but the pressure was extraordinary, and the sight of the bedroom was gone within moments. Some force propelled them through the doorframe and into darkness. The closet door slammed shut behind them. Magia, Luca, and Mateo vanished into the closet. The bedroom was empty.

CHAPTER 4

Luca's, Magia's, and Mateo's bodies somersaulted in the air traveling so quickly they could barely keep their eyes open. The only sounds they could hear were their own shouts for help. Their bodies twisted and squished like they were tumbling through a clothes dryer. Then, within moments, they dropped right down onto what felt like a warm patch of dried grass. The Le Lo Lai that had drawn them into the closet resounded even louder as they came to their senses.

Along with it, the caws of birds and choruses of insects rang. Unlike in Buffalo, the air was warm and moist, almost sweet to the taste. Thick, untamed trees spiraled high and then dropped low overhead. Dazed, the three children each lay in silence.

Luca groaned. "Magia, how on earth did you do—"

He jumped. In his sister's place stood a coquí, the miniature brown tree frog whose loud croak always sang them to sleep. Luca recognized it immediately. They were as common in Puerto Rico as squirrels are in Buffalo. He scrunched his nose at it. What was it doing in Buffalo? And where was his sister? He turned to Mateo and asked, "Mateo, where's Mag—"

In his little brother's place stood a small pig covered in blonde fuzz with a brown streak running from his nose to his pointed ears. The pig blinked up at him with human-like eyes. "Uhm… guys?" Luca took a step back from the two animals and looked around for his siblings. "Where did you go?" he asked. Panic began rising in his throat.

"Luca?" The little frog's voice boomed up at him, disproportionately loud for its tiny body. Luca jumped again. As he landed back on the ground, he noticed the feeling of the dry grass between his toes.

"Where are my…" he looked down for his shoes. But as he craned downward, he saw claw-like bird toes at the end of thin, feathery legs. He stuck his arms out, and in their place, he found a set of wings—rooster wings, with dark, creamy feathers, now flapping frantically. Disbelief drenched the air around him.

The pig, whom Luca now realized was his little brother, began breathing rapidly through his flattened nose. The little coquí frog was the first to speak. "Nobody panic."

"*Nobody panic*?" Luca's crow startled them all. "Magia, what did you *do*?"

"Me?" she shot back, stretching her neck to look up at her brother, who was now much higher above her than usual. She leaped onto a rock to get higher ground. "I didn't do this!" she waved her sticky green toe-hands above her head. She looked around. "Where are we?"

"Don't act like you don't know, Magia."

Mateo laughed. "Yo, rooster—I mean Luca! Pay attention, will ya? We're in the story, of course. This place is Puerto Rico, and I'm a cute little piggy. Isn't this awesome? Checkout my cute curly piggy tail. I can move it with my butt!" Mateo flipped his little tail one way and then the other. Then he tapped his hooves with excitement. He was the only one of them who was amused.

"Well, I hope you like your cute curly tail a whole lot because you might be stuck with it forever, thanks to Magia!" Luca crowed harshly.

"I didn't do this! You think I could do this?" Magia croaked back.

"Yes, you did! You were the one telling the story! You were the one making those sounds!"

"Well..." For once, she struggled to explain. "I honestly don't know what happened. I was telling the story, but the singing and now all this? I wish I could say it was me. Look, I am a good storyteller, but this is more than just a story!" Magia wondered if Luca was also right about this being her fault, somehow.

Mateo's smile faded as he noticed the fear in his sister's voice.

Now Magia was starting to panic. "We can't be in Puerto Rico, Mateo. We live hundreds of miles away from Puerto Rico, yet we were in your room five seconds ago. We were walking toward the closet!"

"Where is the closet?" Luca dashed around, frantically flapping his wings. Even the stench of his rancid baseball gear would be a comfort to him right now.

The three spun around to look for the closet so they could return to the bedroom, but the closet door was gone. In its place stood a tall sign that read *El Yunque National Forest* with a red-colored sticker that said in all caps: CLOSED.

"Huh," Magia looked around. "It looks different from how I remember this place." They then noticed how dry the grass was, how many tree branches lay broken on the ground, how the leaves crackled, and how the lush tree shade had thinned out. It was still vivid and colorful, but it looked as if some event or crisis had drained the life out of it.

El Yunque National Forest: tropical rainforest in Puerto Rico; the only tropical rainforest in the U.S. National Forest System. It's home to hundreds of unique plants and animals, including multiple endangered species.

Mateo walked over to a tree and pulled off the only piece of fruit hanging low from a branch. "Well, we're definitely in Puerto Rico. Do you know how I know for sure? Because they do not have mangos like this in Buffalo! Oh no, in Buffalo, you need ten dollars to buy one mango, and Mami always says they aren't that good!" Mateo took a big bite with his large pig mouth. "Mami was right! These are amazing-licious!"

Mateo plopped down under the mango tree with juicy golden pulp dripping from his snout.

"These are so good!" he squeaked. "You two should try them. You sound like you might be hungry." Magia's eyes widened. Momentarily distracted, her mouth began to water. Oh, how she'd longed for that juicy golden goodness! She hadn't eaten one since they left Puerto Rico.

"I am kind of hungry." Magia hopped over to the mango tree. Mateo pulled off a hunk of mango and handed it to his tiny sister, and she bit into it, skin and all.

"Ahhh," she sighed, slipping into a tropical trance. "This is so good. So sweet and warm and delicious! Oh, I'd become a coquí to have a bite of a mango from Puerto Rico any day! Luca, you should try some of this. They were Papi's favorite!" She sat down, covered in mango juice dripping down her little amphibian face.

Luca wasn't listening. He didn't care about mangos. Luca cared about the fact that he was a rooster—something he did not want to be. He cared about being in Puerto Rico, a place he didn't want to be without his Mami. Luca began panicking and flapping his wings every which way, but he couldn't fly away.

"What the—how do these things work? Why have wings if you can't fly? Useless!" he screeched. "I want to go home—*now!*"

"What do you mean, Luca? Puerto Rico *is* our home," Magia said. She felt a great deal of empathy for him.

"This isn't our home anymore! Our home is in Buffalo!" Luca said.

"But we wanted to return to Puerto Rico," she said.

"Yeah, with Mami and as a *human*! Not without Mami and as a rooster, a pig, and a coquí!"

Hoping to make Luca feel better, Mateo stood up and began to belt out a rap song, making the silliest dance moves as he tried to make Luca laugh. "Luca, eat some mango! *Rico* mango! Eat some mango! Tasty mango! Bite some mango! *Rico* mango! From the tree! Oh yeah! Mateo in da' house, everybody!"

rico: flavorful

It didn't work. Luca glared at him.

They were silent until a strange sound came through the trees.

"Do you hear that?" Magia asked.

Mateo gasped. "It sounds like wings flapping. Maybe it's Godzilla! Or a velociraptor!"

Mateo hid behind Magia, even though he now towered over her in size. Luca slid behind Mateo, even though he was a full head taller than Mateo.

A shadow passed overhead.

"Look in the sky!" Luca cried.

"It's a bird. One that knows how to fly." Mateo snickered.

Luca whacked Mateo on the head with this wing.

Sure enough, a bird was flying in their direction. The three siblings scrambled up together, trying to blend into the landscape.

"Don't worry. I'll keep you safe," Magia said softly. "Let me do the talking."

Mateo whimpered. "What if it tries to eat us?"

"Shhh..." Magia warned, and Mateo and Luca were all too glad to follow her direction.

CHAPTER 5

As the bird got closer, Magia realized this was not just any bird.

"I can't believe it! It's-it's…" she was so excited; she couldn't get the words out.

"A green bird?" Mateo asked innocently.

Luca squinted. The bird also looked familiar, with its velvety green body, red feathers just above his beak, and white rings around his eyes.

"Oh no, that's not just any green bird," Magia said. "That is the Puerto Rican Parrot! He is the most beautiful bird in the world!"

He flew over them, slicing a pathway through the sky. Just as he almost went out of view, he flipped around and turned back, circling the area above them. He was still small in the sky, but he was moving closer. Scanning the earth below, he appeared to be looking for something.

"Shhh, you two," Luca said. "Maybe he won't see us, and he'll leave us alone."

"Why is that bird so special?" Mateo asked. He was still lying low to the ground.

"He's our only parrot native to Puerto Rico and in danger of extinction!" Magia sounded quite concerned.

"*Extinction*?" Mateo asked, worried by her tone.

"Of no longer existing. *La muerte*!" Luca dramatically emphasized every letter of the words, rolling his r's with an eerie timbre that sent shivers down Mateo's spine.

la muerte: death

"Which is why it's even *more* amazing to see one in person!" Magia said.

"Will you two be quiet?" Luca was exasperated. "We don't know if anyone is friendly here."

Mateo gulped. "I hope cute little pigs aren't in danger of extinction!"

He took another careful look through the sky above them.

Magia suddenly propelled herself into the air like popcorn. "Um, hello, Mr. Puerto Rican Parrot," Magia yelled. Her voice seemed to thunder from her petite body.

"Magia!" Luca lunged toward her, trying to contain her beneath his wing. "Right, yell out to him! That's great! You don't know what he'll do to us. And maybe he's not alone!"

Seeing the commotion below, the parrot looked right at them, the whites of his eyes wide. Tucking his glossy wings close to his body, he dove through the air straight toward the kids in the brown, grassy clearing of the forest's entrance. Seeing him closing in, the three clung to one another, preparing for anything. As the parrot neared them, he opened his wings again to catch the wind and float down slowly. With a final flutter, his claw toes landed on the grass with a crunch. He waddled over to them. Seeing them huddled in fear, he gave them a confused look.

"There you are! Sorry, I'm a little late," he said. He fluffed up his silky green, red, and blue feathers.

"Late for what?" Magia asked.

"Ah, *mis amigos*!" The parrot squawked, swept up in excitement. He hopped back and forth to get a good look at the trio as if he were inspecting each one. "Wow, wow, I can't believe it," he said.

mis amigos: my friends

Now that they were closer, the parrot did not seem dangerous. Luca could see the parrot was older than he expected. While his feathers were as vivid and silky as any parrot's, his voice was deep, and his gray beak and toes looked crackly and weathered. As he paced, Luca also noted the parrot's effortlessly confident strut. Luca wondered if he looked like that when he walked, and he puffed his chest to match the parrot's swagger.

"Weren't you expecting me? Who else did you think would meet you here?" the parrot asked.

"Why would we expect you?" Luca replied, losing his patience. "We don't know where we are or what we're doing here!"

Mateo whispered over to his siblings out of the corner of his mouth as he squished grass between his toes. "Does anyone else notice that we are talking to a parrot?"

Luca rolled his eyes. "Says the talking pig!"

"Facts! Ya got me, bro," Mateo said. He giggled as he motioned a fist bump in Lucas's direction and rolled to scratch his back against a fallen branch.

"Call me Pito." The parrot smiled and looked at them with warmth and pride. He reminded Luca of their uncle Rolando who always remembered their birthdays but often lost his glasses on top of his head. The parrot radiated a warmth the kids didn't quite understand.

"Thank you for coming, mis amigos. And not a minute too soon, either. I am so glad to meet you face to face finally. I gotta be honest; my faith was starting to dwindle!"

"I'm sorry, but I don't understand. We didn't expect to be here—this is all a big…" Magia searched for the right word. "Accident! Or some communal hallucination. How could you be expecting us?"

"You responded to my call, didn't you? I mean, it did take you a while, and I was getting very *nervioso*. But you are here now, and that's all that matters." Pito's voice was kind.

nervioso: nervous

Luca interjected. "Um, we didn't respond to your call! We just heard a Le Lo Lai song coming from my closet, so we followed it, and then we—wait." His eyes widened. "Did you teleport us here?"

"Technically, no," Pito said. "The magic transported you here. But I was the one who called for the three of you, Luca."

"The magic?" Luca demanded. "Wait, how do you know my name?"

Pito looked confused. "I know all of your names. Your Papi talked about you constantly."

The children froze. Luca snapped his head to face Pito. "What did you just say? You knew our Papi?"

"Oh, yes. He's the reason you're all here. He passed on the magic."

"What magic?" Magia demanded.

"Ah, amigos, I'm sorry. Now *I'm* confused. I thought your Papi surely told you something of the magic—I know he planned to. You know it. Can't you feel the magic that pulses through our beautiful land? It fills our people, our songs, and our forests—and our food!" he chuckled to himself. "But it can also do other things. And it's how I met your father."

"Stop talking about our father," Luca sneered. "You're a parrot. You could never have known Papi."

Pito flew up to the low branch above the threesome. "This is most unexpected." He rubbed his beak with a wing. "I guess I must teach you about magic if your Papi didn't."

Magia and Mateo moved beneath the branch where Pito sat, like students ready to listen. Luca stood off to the side with a look of suspicion. Pito explained.

"The magic has a way of choosing people. It's a mystery to me, but it chose your father, and it's what allowed him to come here and to help us."

"If this were true, Papi would have told us about it." Luca squinted his eyes at Pito.

"Luca, hear him out," Magia reasoned. "If we learn about the magic, maybe we can get back home."

Luca grumbled but sat down beside his siblings.

Pito began to explain. "Well, it can be confusing and difficult to accept. Not to mention difficult to *control!* The magic has quite a mind of its own. But whenever we needed help, we'd sing the Le Lo Lai song. Your Papi would enter through the closet just like you did. I'm glad it worked with your new bedroom closet too. I wasn't sure since you aren't living in Puerto Rico anymore. *Pero*, alas, the magic of Puerto Rico can find you anywhere!"

"So Papi came through the door just like we did, and that's how you knew him?" Magia asked softly, her eyes wide.

pero: but; however

Pito nodded. "Ay, we were so lucky to have a firefighter who cared about the forest and the island as fiercely as he did. It seemed like no matter the problem, he could figure out how to fix it. I know he planned to tell you about the magic. I guess he didn't have time." Pito's voice trailed off as he said this.

The three stared at him in disbelief. It was all too much for Luca. "Stop talking about Papi as if you knew him! You didn't know him!" Luca stood up again.

Pito's feathers ruffled in the offense. He started to speak but stopped. When he looked into Luca's eyes, he saw tears brimming, and he recognized a reflection of his own loss. "I loved your Papi, and I miss him too."

Mateo wanted to know more—maybe a clue that this bird was telling the truth about being acquainted with his Papi. "Mr. Pito, sir, what did Papi say about us? You said he talked about us."

Turning to Mateo, Pito patted the pig on his snout. "He told me you were funny."

"Really?" asked Mateo. A big piggish grin spread across his face.

"Yes, he did. And he also said you were brilliant. It makes sense that you are a pig—pigs are quite intelligent. Also, observant and persistent, with a big sense of humor."

"You got that right!" Mateo began snorting, holding his head up high.

Pito looked at Magia. "Your Papi said that you are very brave and full of creative ideas. You are the one who always paid attention when your Papi told stories about our beloved Puerto Rico. How fitting that you should be a coquí!"

Magia's mouth turned into a beautiful smile that spread almost the width of her body. "Small frog, big voice," Pito and Magia said simultaneously. Both laughed heartily. It was a common saying in Puerto Rico—everyone marveled at how such a small frog could be loud enough to sing for a whole village.

"Yup, that's me!" she said. Her little coquí chest rounded with Puerto Rican pride.

Finally turning to Luca, Pito said, "And he told me you're also an extremely proud *puertorriqueño.* That you love baseball and always tell it like it is—a truth-teller." The parrot looked deep into Luca's eyes. "It makes sense that you're a rooster—the symbol of masculinity, but gentle and protective of his flock, keeping the people on track by waking us all up in the morning." Luca felt a bit of a poke inside his chest, a heaviness that seemed familiar. He didn't know how to handle this stranger bird telling him all these things his Papi said.

puertrriqueño: Puerto Rican

Magia was unsure how Luca would respond to this and decided to change the subject. "Did Papi come as an animal too? He must have been something big and strong and majestic!"

"Ah," Pito leaned in, clearly pleased by the question. "Your Papi was a *pitirre.*" He almost whispered as if he were telling them a great secret. When the kids cocked their heads, Pito tossed his head back in disbelief. "The Gray Kingbird! The most Puerto Rican of all birds—well, maybe besides me. Small in stature but *big* in courage. Never afraid!"

pitirre: the Gray Kingbird, known for chasing down larger predators like hawks despite its small size

"Our dad was a…tiny little bird?" Luca stammered.

"Not just a little bird, *mijo*. Every creature of the forest, even the guaraguao hawk, scurries away in the presence of a pitirre. How fitting that your Papi was the rainforest pitirre. He was the definition of courage and service," Pito said with excitement and a hint of sadness. "Your Papi told me he'd pass his magic to you three."

mijo: an affectionate term meaning "my son"

"If only we knew anything about this so-called magic!" Luca said.

Pito turned to Luca, shoulders squared with each other. "Well, you are a rooster. Your sister is a coquí, and your brother is a pig! You may know nothing about the magic, but clearly the magic knows about you. You're very bright children, and I believe you'll catch on. And there's a reason I called you."

The kids eyed him with curiosity. "You see, there is big trouble that no one on the island has been able to fix. Not the humans, not the forest, and none of the animals."

Luca squawked. "No, no, no. *We're* the ones who need help! We want to go back home!"

Pito shook his head. "I don't have that power. The thing about the magical closet is that I can call you here, and you can ignore it or choose to come. But the magic decides when you're ready to go home. I can't control that part."

Luca lowered his head and began tapping his feet back and forth in panic. "What do you mean you can't control *that* part? The part as in going back home? That part?"

Luca plopped down on the ground and folded his wings. "What could you possibly need from *us*?"

CHAPTER 6

Pito motioned with his wing.

"Just look around and see for yourself."

When they first arrived, the children noticed it seemed unusual. But now, they looked more closely and saw just how bad it was.

Magia said, "I remember coming to the forest with Papi, and it seemed so different." She looked around and remembered the rainforest's sense of charm. So different from what they all saw around them now. El Yunque used to burst forth with colors, sights, and sounds of its own design. Deep magenta flowers, bulbs of yellow mango, and more shades of green than one could ever count. A symphony of croaking frogs, shrieking birds, and buzzing insects all created their own celebratory rhythmic cadence. Even the trees seemed to pulse with low base notes. The deep, earthy smell of soil and vegetation used to fill their lungs.

But not anymore. Now, the vibrant greens had turned pale yellow and brown. Any fruit or flower left was lying on the ground, mostly crushed. Trees lay on their sides, roots ripped out of the earth, and reaching up to the sky for help. Those still standing had been stripped of their leaves. The tallest trees used to shield hikers in a luxurious shade covering, but now most of them were bent over as if carrying a burden too heavy to bear. While insects and animals still buzzed and rustled, the sound was lower and slower, like they were dragging their feet. The once vibrant ecosystem was now veiled by gloom and the blistering sun. All that remained were memories of what once was and might never be again.

Mateo asked, "Isn't the forest supposed to be a majestic place? What happened? It's not looking very royal!"

Pito explained, "That's why I called you. Come with me, and I'll show you how bad it has gotten." Pito bent down and said, "Magia, jump on my back, and you boys follow me on the ground."

Magia hopped on the bird's back and held on with her sticky fingers and tocs. Up they went, and Magia could see over the top of the massive rain forest. It looked even more barren looking down on the forest from the sky. Magia wondered where the animals were going to live.

Below, logs and branches piled up in the pathways making it very hard for Mateo and Luca to progress. But slowly, they made their way to the center of the rainforest. The walking paths were almost impossible to see—if Pito had not been leading them, they easily could have lost their way.

"Are we there yet?" Mateo whined, struggling over a large branch.

Luca looked back at him. "We've only been walking for five minutes."

"Yeah, but right now, I'm a roasting, hungry pig, and that is not a good thing! I ain't about this hiking rainforest life!" Mateo responded with a breathy pause in his voice.

"I'm pretty sure you were hungry before we even got here," Luca added.

"Well, kids," Pito interrupted, "we are here."

As he said this, he dipped low beneath one last branch before reaching an open clearing. In the center of the clearing was a giant tree, spiraling and sprawling over them.

After a few moments, Mateo asked, "Is that a Flamboyan?"

Pito nodded.

"The street where we used to live had Flamboyans everywhere," Magia said. Shaped like umbrellas, the kids used to lean up against them for shade as they ate their piraguas after school with their Papi. The fiery red blossoms covered almost the entire tree until the dome of the tree looked just like their cherry-flavored shaved ice. This one was ancient, one of the biggest they'd ever seen.

"What's-what's wrong with her?" Luca asked. He stared up at her from her base.

She was obviously the star as if this clearing was her stage. But she didn't look okay. Rather than standing strong and tall, her trunk was leaning over, and her branches, bare and quivering, were stripped of flowers and leaves. While Flamboyans' branches are usually brimming with wildlife, this one could hardly hold herself, let alone any other creatures. It was shocking to see a tree so majestic and so lifeless at the same time.

Pito continued. "Before the hurricanes, her branches were like paintbrushes coloring the blue skies with a vibrant red bursting into shades of purple. It was, *muy bello*. But her blossoms are gone, and her body has become barren, pale, and weak."

All the other trees around her were in the same state, either fallen or bent over, and they looked like they were in mourning.

muy bello:
very beautiful

"What happened here?" Magia asked.

"Do you know about the two hurricanes that destroyed our lovely island?" Pito asked.

Luca nodded his head. "Mami told us all about it. She said Hurricane Irma was a powerful hurricane—a category five!"

Mateo asked, "Is five a bad number?"

"For hurricanes, it is. It's the worst it could be," Luca said.

"And then Hurricane Maria landed here two weeks later as a category four!" Pito said. Fear filled the air with a sense of despair and hopelessness. "The two hurricanes combined destroyed so much of the island! It caused dangerous flooding, damaged the electrical plants, and left everyone in the dark."

"I remember that Mami said people were trapped in their homes and couldn't leave for weeks!" Magia answered. "Mami didn't like to watch it on the news too long because it made her so sad."

Hurricanes Irma & Maria: In September of 2017, Puerto Rico was struck by two major hurricanes within two weeks of each other.

Pito said, "The Puerto Rican people are strong, just like the trees, animals, and every living thing that grows here. We'd be rebuilding now if we'd suffered only one terrible hurricane. But the entire island suffers from shock, having had the second one come so soon after the first. The damage is devastating, and it's hard to even know where to start with the rebuilding. The rainforest especially was shaken at its very core. Some of its oldest trees were uprooted, and now the forest is overexposed to the sun."

Luca looked around and couldn't believe the rainforest had been through so much. He could almost feel the ache of the trees as they tried their hardest to provide shade, but they just couldn't. The people of Puerto Rico had lost so much, and the island was in despair. Part of him almost forgot how far they were from home.

"Not to be rude, but how can we possibly help with any of this?" Luca genuinely wanted to know.

"Well, we always used to call your Papi in moments like this. We need help—we need *your* help. You see, none of us parrots can rebuild our homes in the branches of the trees as long as they are all bent over. This Flamboyan is our matriarch, the oldest and tallest. She has given birth to dozens of smaller trees around her and provided a home to young parrots just like me for decades upon decades. She is particularly special to me." Pito looked up at her with mist in his eyes. "Because my abuela raised me in this tree."

There was a long silence.

Magia spoke up, "But surely Puerto Rico can rebuild. We are a strong people, and the rainforest and the Flamboyans have survived many hurricanes. I don't understand."

Pito shook his head. "That's why I called you and brought you to the Flamboyan. The tree has lost all her leaves, flowers, and small branches, but that's not the worst part."

Mateo asked, "What could be worse?"

Pito looked as sad as a parrot could look. "She has lost hope. When she lost hope, so did the rest of the island. When she gave up, everyone and everything did too. You see, the forest is the heart of Puerto Rico, and Flamboyan is the heart of the forest. We need her to inspire us all. Without hope, all is lost."

The trio listened with concern. Luca hung his head, feeling so small beneath the majestic tree in mourning. He shifted uncomfortably.

Pito bobbed his slender head, and his feathers glistened. "Sometimes the sadness makes me feel like the forest will never be green again."

After a few more moments of silence, Pito suddenly opened his beak and let out an ear-splitting shriek. Far off in the distance, a swirling black pillar of smoke came into view. It looked like a tornado, but it never touched the ground, and spun around in all directions. The closer it came, the bigger it grew. The bigger it grew, the greener it looked.

They were instantly engulfed in a feather tornado as dozens of parrots flew around their heads. Just as abruptly, they all landed on the twisted and broken branches of the trees above them.

"You called?" one of the parrots inquired.

Pito wrung his wings. "I called the three children of Papi Pitirre, our past protector. I've asked them to help us. I know they have the magic, just like their Papi. I can feel it in my feathers, and my feathers have never failed me. But..." Pito stopped and the parrots leaned in close to hear the following words. "...they know *nothing* about the magic."

"Nothing?" one of the parrots gasped.

"Nothing."

This time, all the birds gasped. Then, the air erupted with the ear-splitting chorus that can only occur with a flock of upset parrots.

"They know nothing at all about the magic?"

"How can that be?"

"What will we do now?"

"How can they possibly help?"

"Silence!" Pito's voice sliced through the squawks, and there was quiet.

"You all listen to me right now. The children may not know about the magic, but they are the only ones who can help us. Papi Pitirre said we could call them to help, and he never lied to us."

Magia hopped up beside Pito. "Pito is right. We may not know about the magic, but here we are, and our Papi must have passed on the magic for a reason. We will figure out how to help the rain forest. In fact, we'll figure out how to help all of Puerto Rico."

Luca shot her a surprised look; feathers splayed around his head like a lion's mane. "We can't even figure out how to get ourselves home, Magia. How will we ever save even one tree, let alone *all* of Puerto Rico?" Luca looked to Mateo for an ally, but Mateo was bobbing his snout in agreement beside Magia.

One of the parrots called out to the flock. "They must have been brought here for *some* reason," the parrot sighed.

Another bobbed his head up and down. "Yes, we could always trust their Papi."

"What about the stone?" one parrot squawked.

CHAPTER 7

"The stone? Are you kidding us? The stone means nothing," a parrot in the group said. Others called out their own feelings.

"That's just old folktale stuff!"

"It's a dead end, my friend."

"Could be some ancient ping-pong ball for all we know!"

Pito spoke out again. "What other options do we have? We've never known what it says before, and maybe they can read it."

Still standing at the base of the Flamboyan, the kids looked at each other nervously. One of the parrots stepped forward with a semi-rounded stone in his mouth. It was roughly the size of a silver dollar, with smooth irregular edges and small weathered carvings on its surface. He released it from his grip and placed it on the ground before them. The three kids gathered around it so they could see the ancient symbols scratched into the rock.

Pito explained. "It is said that these rocks were carved by the Taino, the indigenous people of our island."

"We are part Taino!" Mateo offered eagerly.

"Yes, we have Taino ancestry, and Papi told me about them," Magia said. "Give me a moment and let me try to remember what he said."

"As if some rock is going to make a difference." Luca turned away.

Magia smiled. "It's coming back to me—what Papi told me. Many years ago, before the Europeans came and brought enslaved Africans, the Taino people etched prophecies into rocks all over the island. Almost like they knew a change was coming and wanted to write letters to preserve their legacy through whatever would come." She looked up at the parrot. "Where did you find this?"

The parrot said, "I found this one after Hurricane Maria. The hurricane washed away some soil around Flamboyan, and I found this in her roots. The strange markings caught my eye, so I pulled it out. I wanted to see what it said."

A parrot in the crowd mocked him. "Only parrots can't read human writing."

The parrot looked down, a bit embarrassed, then turned toward the three siblings. "Well, true. But what about you? You're human. Can you read what it says?"

Magia, Luca, and Mateo continued to circle the stone. Suddenly, a grin spread across Magia's tiny coquí face.

"I remember a story Papi used to tell us. When we were little and all shared a room, he'd tuck us in, open our window so a cool breeze could waft through, and we would listen to the crickets and coquís as he'd tell us stories about Taino legends."

"Yeah, I remember those." Luca stepped up, emboldened by a memory of his own. "And sometimes, when we were waiting at a restaurant, he'd take the crayons and draw symbols on the napkins, then we'd have to guess what they meant."

The three studied the stone, their eyes adjusting to the circuitous way the Tainos used lines to illustrate pictures and string them together. So much different from the rigid, individual letters of English they scribbled with their pencil in school. These symbols, they imagined, took a lot longer to make. So, the writer needed to be clear yet creative—getting right to the point but lacing as much meaning into each line as possible.

Luca squinted as his brain began to connect the dots between these strange lines and the real world. The kids suddenly looked at each other.

Magia spoke up. "That is a pig, a rooster, and a coquí—it's us!"

Luca snatched the stone with his rooster claw toes. "Give me that! You missed something. There's also, well, a person coming out of a mountain." Looking up, he asked, "What could that mean?"

The parrots burst into clatter and whistles.

"He's not even real!"

"I told you, an old folktale!"

Pito put up his wing for silence. "I know you don't believe in the prophecies, but be still and let the children see if their magic will reveal a secret."

Magia confirmed. "It does look like a man is coming out of the mountain."

"That's one of our legends," Pito explained. "Do you see that mountain over there? It's said that the mountain is where The Sleeping Giant lives. If you look closely, you can see his shape."

Sure enough, on the far right was a head with a nose, sloping down into a chest and back up with his legs, like he was laying on a reclining chair.

Magia shared more. "I remember stories about him, and that Papi said his real name was 'Yukahú.' He was over twenty feet tall, with dark skin and straight black hair down past his shoulders." And as if a riddle had been solved by Magia mentioning his name, a green glow suddenly surrounded the stone.

The parrots, Luca, and Mateo gasped in awe.

"¡*Wepa*! There you go! You're getting your magic already!" Pito said.

"I am?" Magia basked in the green glow.

"Yes!" Pito said. "Yukahú is the protector of the rainforest. Once he gave the job of

wepa: a celebratory word used by Puerto Ricans to exclaim joy; yay!

caring for the island to the humans, he laid down on the forest floor and went to sleep."

"Aren't we forgetting there is no *real* sleeping giant?" a parrot asked. "This can't be the answer to our problems."

Pito looked so discouraged. "I want to believe that he is real, and that he will help the rainforest grow again."

Magia was sure Yukahú was the answer to this riddle. Magia put her coquí arms on her coquí hips and stamped her coquí foot. "Look, I think the stone is a prophecy. And we're in it. Besides, we're stuck here until this *magic* or whatever decides to bring us back home. We love our people and our island. And it's in trouble. *You're* in trouble. If this is what our Papi normally would have done, then we must try at least. Let's go find the Sleeping Giant and do whatever we can to wake him up!"

Luca hesitated but then, agreeing with Magia for once, said what they all wanted to say. "Maybe he can help us get back home too! If anyone can."

Pito nodded his head. "Truth be told, it will be a long journey up to the top."

Parrots began yelling out. "This is stupid. Count me out!"

"Me, too!"

"They're fools."

And with that, the parrots became a funnel of feathers swirling around the tree, and then flew off in a messy mob into the sky and out of sight. The kids craned their necks watching as they left.

"Whoa," Mateo gasped.

"Forget them," Magia said. "If we've got magic, then let's use it."

"Who says we have any magic?" Luca asked. He furrowed his feathery brows.

"We'll have to figure it out along the way." Magia croaked and hopped up on Mateo's back. Pito was the only parrot left as the small group set out on their journey. Above them, Pito led the way.

CHAPTER 8

Luca's stomach was churning. So much was happening at once! First Mami left, then the closet transported them to Puerto Rico, and now the mountain might be an actual sleeping giant!

"Magia!" Luca called out loudly. "We should have a plan before we try to wake up a snoring, sleepy giant who could drown us with his drool before we ever get back to Buffalo! I'm just saying!"

"If the hike is so long, we'll have plenty more time to figure it out along the way! I'm just saying!" Magia said.

"C'mon Luca!" Mateo nudged him.

Luca squawked, bothered. "Why does everyone always take her side? I'm the man of the house, after all."

"Well, I'm the woman-of-the-good-ideas. And we're not in the house, we're in the forest. We need to get rolling if we're going to make it in time. You do want to go back home, right?" Magia asked. She was sassy but with an honest flare.

The trail was visible now, with lots of fallen branches and pools of water to navigate around. After a short while, the three siblings started to feel like they were melting. Their bodies had forgotten how to handle the Caribbean sun.

"How did we ever live in this heat? I'm boiling!" Luca said.

"I know! I think my butt is sweating!" Mateo yelled.

"Thank you for that lovely image. Now I'm traumatized." Luca shook his head in disgust.

Magia was also missing the Buffalo snow right now, though she would never admit it out loud. She was supposed to be Puerto Rican—*boricua* through and through. She didn't like to think that Buffalo may have changed her, even a little.

boricua: a person from Puerto Rico. This word comes from a Taino word, so Puerto Ricans use it to honor their island's heritage.

"You know what I'm thinking sounds good? A piragua! The best invention to combat heat!" Mateo drooled as he imagined sticking his snout into that decadent cup of shaved ice, the Puerto Rican snow cone.

"I want a mango piragua!" he yelled. He seemed to think if he said it loud enough, a *piraguero* might show up with a piragua cart.

piraguero: a person who sells piraguas, usually from a cart

"And I'll take a *piragua de coco,*" Magia said, excitedly playing along.

"*De guava, por favor.*" Luca chimed in with his order, forgetting for a moment that he was stuck in the rainforest.

piragua de coco: coconut-flavored piragua

The trio tripped, climbed, hopped, and stumbled over fallen debris as the night got darker, and the trail became messier. They savored the beams of moonlight that slipped through the trees to light the way. But over time, it became so dark they could hardly see each other—especially with Magia being so small at the lead and Pito flying overhead. They continued chatting, not so much to make conversation but more to eliminate the possibility of losing track of one another.

de guava, for favor: guava-flavored, please

"I wonder what time it is and what Tía Clara is doing back home—probably watching *novelas.*" Magia wondered out loud.

novelas: soap operas

"Maybe she's thinking about how we're going to wake up a *massive*, sleeping, rainforest giant," Luca said. Sarcasm was rapidly becoming his third language.

"Do you think we're going to make it on time? I'm getting hungry! I want to make it home on time for dinner." Mateo worried about the simpler things.

Luca was scared, but trying to stay calm—at least in this instance. He thought about how self-possessed his Papi was in dangerous situations. He dealt with danger at work all the time. But he always protected and saved others, putting their lives before his own. Even at home when everything was chaotic, he never lost his cool. Luca wanted to be like Papi.

They trekked on, drenched in sweat and mist, keeping an eye on Pito as he guided them on their way. No matter how many times Mateo asked, "Are we there yet?" there was no way for any of them to know. The uphill path grew steeper, but the foliage was too thick to see how far they'd come or how long they had left.

They continued, chattering on as the heat lost its intensity. With the night came a haze that settled over everything around them. Beneath it all, the coursing water of the *Río Espíritu Santo* roared louder under the reign of the moon and the silence of the stars. It was deafening.

Río Espíritu Santo: Holy Spirit River; the large river that runs through El Yunque rainforest

The darker it got, the jumpier Luca was. Mateo followed mere inches behind Magia with large, spooked eyes, almost stepping on her now and then. Magia was good at looking brave, but she, too, was growing nervous seeing her brothers so afraid. After her dad died, Magia promised herself that she would always take care of her brothers. She learned if there are too many tears, everything falls apart. Magia wasn't sure how many was too many, but she never wanted to find out again. She would take care of it, so the boys would never find out again. She took one last deep breath and plastered on a brighter attitude.

"Let's stop here for the night, boys."

"I'm so tired," Mateo said.

Luca was just plain cranky. "I agree. Let's get some sleep."

Pito landed on a thorny branch on a twisted tree in the clearing. The three found soft places to curl up, and soon, they were all fast asleep.

Early the following day, as the sun just started cresting the horizon, Luca unexpectedly awoke earlier than he ever had, and he was ready to begin his day. *Great! Now I'm a rooster and I can't sleep in even if I want too.*

He stood up, a bit achy from the first night he'd ever slept as a rooster, and his first thought was to wake the others up with a loud cock-a-doodle-doo. He liked the idea of annoying his siblings, especially Magia, but felt bad doing it to Pito. Besides that, he didn't feel like talking to anyone yet. Instead, he started pecking around for something to eat.

As he pecked, he mumbled to himself. *I don't want to climb that stupid mountain to help those parrots anyway. Or the forest, either, for that matter. I want to find the closet and get out of here.* He pecked harder and harder at the tender ground, his stomach grumbling.

Ugh! There's nothing good to eat here in this stupid forest! He stomped his feet as he wandered further to see what else he could find. In his irritation, he didn't realize that he had gone a long way. But when he realized he could no longer see the others, his irritation turned to panic. *I am lost.*

"Magia? Mateo? Magia! Mateo!" he yelled, trotting in circles. All the trees looked the same. Ordinarily, Luca did everything he could to avoid thinking about Papi. But this morning, he kept wondering what Papi would do if he were here. He whispered a desperate plea. *Papi, I need your help*!

Luca didn't hear his father's voice, but he heard something else. Music.

CHAPTER 9

While he usually would have been wary of a strange musician in the middle of the forest, he wanted with everything in him at that moment to get out of this forest.

"It was a song that got us here, and maybe another song can get us out," he said to himself.

Without stopping to think, Luca took off and ran as fast as he could toward the music—toward the angelic gentle strumming of strings. Over the fallen logs, under low-hanging branches, through the mud and moss, the sound became louder and louder. Clearly, it was a guitar, but not just any guitar! This stringed instrumental music he heard was the sound of a cuatro—Papi's favorite Puerto Rican instrument! He took it as a sign. Running toward the music meant running deeper into the forest where there wasn't even a little trail to follow.

As Luca became more disoriented, his confidence began to falter, and a pang of guilt set in for leaving his siblings. *What if I can't find them again? What if they wake up and see I'm gone? They'll be so worried. What if I find the door, but they can't get home because they're not here?* Now he felt like the worst brother of all, but his curiosity was piqued, and most of all, he desperately wanted to get back home. He continued moving toward the beautiful melodic sounds of the cuatro.

Luca intended to sneak up quietly and see who was playing that cuatro before he could be seen. But as he was about to enter the clearing where the rhythmic sounds were coming from, he tripped over a vine and tumbled out into the open. Opposite him, a reptilian creature stood on its hind legs, its long tail falling to the leafy floor behind. The pale-green dinosaur-like skin of the iguana glistened in the shafts of light that peeked between the leaves. But he didn't look like any iguana Luca had ever seen. This one wore a crisp white *guayabera* and loose white pants like a true *jíbaro* of Puerto Rico.

guayabera: a light, usually short-sleeved shirt, which has buttons, pleats, and large pockets down the front.

Luca braced himself, but to his surprise, the iguana ignored him. He went on tuning his small cuatro—a stringed instrument, sort of a mix between a mandolin and a guitar. When the notes were just right, the little creature tipped his straw hat toward Luca. He looked exactly like the men who would perform in the town plazas, playing their instruments and attracting large crowds to play and sing along as others watched and played dominoes. Now sitting up and taking in the musician's entire appearance, Luca attempted to keep himself from laughing. That's when the iguana spoke.

jíbaro: a Puerto Rican farmer from the mountains; also used to describe a person who is proud of their Puerto Rican roots.

"Have you come for the show, *Señor Gallo*?"

Luca blinked. "Are you—"

"*El gran cantante, Guan Anthony*? Why yes! I am the resident singer and performer in this part of the rainforest. I see you've heard of me!"

Señor Gallo: Mr. Rooster

el gran cantante: the grand singer

"Not really," Luca said under his breath, not wanting to get on this little reptile's wrong side. He opted for: "You're an iguana."

"Well, you, my rooster friend, are a *gran* observer! Even if that *is* the understatement of the century. Please, call me Guanito. Take your seat. The performance is about to begin."

gran: grand; great

Luca froze.

"Aren't you going to sit?"

"Excuse me, Mr. Guanito, sir," Luca said, "but I didn't come here for the show. Though I'm sure your performance is really something! I came here for directions. You see, I'm lost. I shouldn't be here."

Guanito looked incredulous. "You didn't come to hear my performance?"

Luca felt sorry for the musician. He knew how it felt when no one wanted to hear him play his trumpet. "I just meant… I found you by accident, but now that I am here, I would love to hear you play."

The iguana perked up instantly.

"But first, could you tell me where I am?"

Guanito strummed his cuatro with enthusiasm. "*Sí*, of course, my new friend. You are in El Yunque!"

sí: yes

"Yes, of course, I am. But *where* in El Yunque?"

The iguana put his head next to Luca's. "Excuse me, but whatever do you mean? We're in the rainforest. Simple as that."

Luca's face dropped, unable to hide his despair. "Ugh, I'm doomed! I will never find my way back!"

"Ah, perhaps knowing where you came *from* may help us solve your problem. Where exactly did you come from?" Guanito asked him.

"I was with my sister and brother."

"And they were…where?" Guanito continued questioning.

Luca sighed again. "I don't know where we were. Or where they are either."

Guanito thought for a long minute. "So, you don't know where you are. You don't know where you've been. You don't know where your brother and sister are. And you don't know where you want to go? You sound very troubled. I think the best thing to do is to sit down here by the river and forget about it until the sun comes up."

"But I don't want to forget about getting home! And I don't want to forget about my family! I need help getting back! I need to know where the cl—"

"Is there more to forget about than being lost?" Guanito interrupted Luca with drama and Spanish flamenco flare in his voice as he strummed his tiny cuatro passionately.

"Do you know about the magic?" Luca asked. He sighed deeply. "Everybody here seems to know about the magic and my Papi and—"

"Si amigo, I do know about *the* magic. But your Papi? I have no clue." Guanito suddenly made the connection. "Wait! Do you mean *Papi Pitirre*?" the iguana asked.

"You knew him too?" Luca was shocked.

"He was our protector, and we all knew him." Guanito nodded. "I can't believe you are his son! Actually, yes, I can! Being out here, without knowing where you are or where you are going, but still wanting to get somewhere and find your family—that is a brave thing. I see you take after him."

Luca coughed away an emotion rising in his long, feathered throat. "You know what I want to do? If the magic is true, I want to use it to be more like my Papi. I want to be strong, fight hawks, and help people—and always know what to do."

"Oh, but your Papi's greatest strength came from his heart! He was brave and kind. It's okay to be sad and miss your Papi, you know." Guanito spoke with compassion as he strummed his cuatro.

Luca sat silently for a moment as if he hadn't heard Guanito. "I'd also use the magic to become a professional baseball player like Roberto Clemente and get in the Hall of Fame!" He chuckled, but he realized Guanito was still looking at him with a thoughtful expression from beneath the rim of his straw hat and over the edge of his glasses.

"But I'd only do that if there was a little extra magic to spare. Right now, I'd mostly use it to find my siblings again. Magic or no magic, can you help me?"

Guanito nodded and smiled.

CHAPTER 10

Mateo yawned and stretched out his short legs.

"Oh, I'm so stiff. I don't think pigs were meant to sleep in the rainforest."

He stood up and looked around. Sleeping beside him was Magia, curled up in a little ball. Across from them, Pito slept on a fallen branch. And Luca... wait! *Where was Luca?*

"Wake up, Magia!" Mateo shook his sister. "Luca is gone!"

"Stop shaking me!" Magia protested. "Luca is what?"

"He's gone, Magia!"

Pito woke from the yelling beneath him. He perched on his branch and scanned the forest nearby. "You are right, little pig. I don't see him!"

Magia was instantly awake. "Luca!" she yelled. The other two joined her, screaming at the top of their lungs. But there was no response.

Pito flew overhead. "I can see his claw prints. They go downstream along the curvy river."

Magia crossed her arms in desperation. She was upset with herself for losing track of her brother. "How are we ever going to find him? We'll never catch up!"

Pito smiled. "Ah, that's not the case. You can float down the river until you see him—it will be easy."

Mateo frowned. "Easy for you, maybe. But I'm a pig. If you haven't noticed, these stumpy legs aren't natural-born paddlers! I don't even know how to swim, like, in real life."

"Hmm." Pito thought for a moment. "Maybe yes. Maybe no. Until you try, you'll never know!"

"Well, you'd better not sink because I'm going to be riding on your head!" Magia said. "Come on! You can do this!"

Mateo didn't realize it, but he was holding his breath, almost passing out, before reaching the river shore. Magia noticed and reminded him to breathe as she scampered up to his head and commanded him to get into the water.

He waded into the water, where it was shallow and calm. "I will just walk along the edge like this."

But Pito flew up behind him, scaring him so that he fell into the white, frothy current. Mateo squealed.

"Relax! You can float!" cried Magia.

"I'm sinking!" shrieked Mateo. His head was just about to sink beneath the rapids when a green glow surrounded his body. Without effort, he floated back to the top as if his body was an inner tube filled with air.

"It's magic!" Pito called from the air. "See, you do have it after all! You might not know the magic, but the magic sure knows you!"

Magia giggled and held onto her brother's ears for balance. Together, they careened down the river, squealing in delight.

It wasn't long before Pito hollered to them, "Hush, listen! I hear something."

The siblings glided silently along the current. "I hear it too," Magia said.

Mateo gasped. "It sounds like a cuatro playing."

Magia used Mateo's ears for steering, stretching out her hind coquí legs just enough to grip the edge of his ears and point him in the right direction.

"Pull over to the shore, Mateo."

Mateo pulled over ever so carefully, hoping this magic thing didn't run out before he got out of the water.

"Hold on, Magia! We're coming in for a landing! This might get bumpy!" Mateo yelled, half joking, half serious.

Magia was holding onto Mateo's ears for dear life when she spotted something in the distance.

Magia spotted Luca on the shore. "I think I see him! Turn, turn!" With surprising ease and precision, Mateo angled his body and floated them up to the river's edge.

Crawling out of the water, Mateo walked dripping toward his brother with Magia still on his head. They called to Luca, and when he turned around, they caught a glimpse of Guanito and heard his beautiful music.

Guanito paused for a moment, then bowed. "Is this your sister and brother, Luca?"

Luca ran towards them with an uncharacteristic lightness in his step.

"I'm so glad to see you!" he wrapped them in a feathery hug, the soft inner side of his feathers tickling them. Magia and Mateo looked at each other, confused by Luca's chipper disposition.

Magia started in on him. "Why did you wander off, Luca? We were so worried about you! You think you can wander off in the wee hours of the—"

"I'm sorry I left," he apologized before she could even finish, which completely threw her off. "I'm sorry I made you worry. I won't do it again. But there's someone I want you to meet. Come meet el gran cantante, Guan Anthony! Better known as Guanito."

Magia pulled herself up as tall as she could. "Oh, forgive me, sir."

Guanito bowed deeply. "Nothing to forgive. It is an honor, *hermosa* coquí!"

hermosa: gorgeous

"*Mi nombre es Magia*," she clarified.

mi nombre es: my name is

"Ah, Magia. And you?"

"Mateo."

"I am Guanito, renowned in all of the rainforest for playing Puerto Rico's beloved instrument, el cuatro."

Pito looked a little starstruck. "Guanito, it is very nice to meet you in person finally! Your fame precedes you!"

"Not to be rude," Magia turned from Guanito back to the others, "but seriously, Luca, I'm glad you made a friend. I am. But now we're even further from the mountaintop. And we've lost the trail. Pito, do you know how to get back on it? I don't want to spend another night here. It's a little scary."

"Scary? Did you say scary, Magia?" Luca was surprised his sister used this word. She was the bravest person he knew, after Papi, that is. But he would never let her know.

"Oh great! We're doomed! Magia is scared! Our Captain is down! Our ship is sinking!" Mateo was extremely agitated.

"I'm okay, brothers. I want to sleep in my bed tonight, that's all." Magia shrugged, trying to make light of it.

"Where is it you are trying to go again? Up the mountain?" Guanito asked.

"Well," Pito considered whether to tell this small reptile of their plans. "The truth is, we are going to find The Sleeping Giant, Yukahú. Many believe he is folklore, at best, and someone who has let us down, at worst. Call me old-fashioned, but I believe he is there. I can't explain it, but I believe if we can get these kids to him, he will be able to help us recover from all this."

"I know what you mean, friend. And I do not judge you for your hope," Guanito nodded solemnly to Pito. "As a matter of fact, I may be able to help. Pito, you know the skies and the large trails you can see from them. But I know the forest floor. I know the hidden paths you cannot see with an untrained eye. I can lead you all the fastest, most direct way up to the top."

"And I can finish my concert along the way," Guanito added. "I haven't had much of an audience since the hurricanes. My rainforest friends have not been much in the mood for music." Guanito flashed a big smile. "How about it?"

The kids and Pito all nodded to one another. Guanito serenaded his newfound friends as they hiked to the mountain top.

Magia, Luca, and Mateo thought the path Pito had led them on before was rough. It was a hiking path humans used, but with fallen debris and obstacles to avoid. In comparison to the one they were on, that one felt like a red carpet. Guanito's path was not a path at all, at least not one you could see with the naked eye. It had to be *sensed* by someone who had traveled it a million times but had left no trace to give away the secret avenue. Luckily, that was Guanito. Unluckily, the kids hurdled and heaved over boulders, under branches, around leaves, through tall grasses, over slippery moss, and through pointy bushes until they were out of breath and soaked in sweat.

"This is worse than the worst P.E. class ever! I am going to hurl. If I don't have six-pack abs after all this torture, I want a refund!" Mateo grunted, rolling himself over another scraggly fallen tree.

"Mateo—" Luca started.

"No, I'm serious. Everyone's all like, 'Oh, Mateo is so go-with-the-flow, so handsome, never bothered by anything. He's always happy and funny.' But seriously, guys, I have my limits and this is—"

"Mateo!" they all shouted at him in unison.

"What?"

"I think we're here," Guanito announced, standing upright on his back legs. Just as they took a few more steps up the incline, they saw a massive form emerging behind it. Looking as if it had been carved into the mountain centuries ago, the very top of the mountain rose before them. Roots and vines grew from the sides; moss was all over it. As they looked at it from just enough distance, they could make out the contours of a man's face in the stone, multiple stories high, laying on his back, facing toward the sky.

CHAPTER 11

Pito trembled as he flew toward the rocky features.

"This has to be him—it has to be him," he whispered reverently. "They were all wrong. This must be him!" Pito sounded a little crazy, except that they were all seeing it.

The kids, and even Guanito, approached with cautious steps, quietly inching forward toward the enormous stony figure. Looking to the left, they could see the dip of his neck, rise of his chest, and expanse of his legs stretching further down the ridge of the mountain.

At that moment, a soft green glow began to ripple across the mountain. No one could deny it.

"This is it," Magia said. "The prophecy was right. This mountain has to be it. I think we're beginning to get the hang of this magic business!"

Everyone was so happy! They danced, sang, and celebrated. Luca was the only one who didn't join the fun. "Um, hello? We never figured out how to wake him up! If only I had my trumpet, maybe that could wake him up."

"We're planning to wake him up, bro, not scare him half to *deaf*." Mateo teased his brother, thinking himself quite clever for his play on words. Luca scowled at him.

"Don't worry. I have an idea!" Mateo turned his hat around, jumped on a log, and excitedly began to rap. "We found a giant! Taking a nap! Time to wake him up! How about that! Sleeping time is over! No more z's allowed! C'mon friends, let's get loud!"

"That's a great idea, Mateo! Let's yell and see if that does the trick." Magia was open to any suggestion.

They joined their voices and screamed out, "Wake up! Wake up! Wake up!" The eyelids of the giant remained shut as if they hadn't made any noise at all. Their yells faded once again into a quiet disappointment.

Magia looked around gathering ideas for a new plan.

"I've got an idea," Magia said. "There are pebbles all around here. Let's gather a bunch and toss them at the giant. He's made of stone, so it won't hurt him. Maybe he just needs a little shake."

Luca rolled his eyes. He was fed up with this nonsense. "There's no way I'm throwing rocks at the side of a mountain as if it will wake up and turn into a man."

Tat. Tat. Tat. The others hurled pebbles from the ground around them, and they bounced off the giant's cheek and shoulder and chest as if the rocks were nothing but flies.

When the group had thrown the last pebble, Magia, Mateo, and Pito sat down on a fallen log.

"Now, what are we going to do? He's still sleeping!" Mateo moaned. "Maybe we can't do this after all!"

Magia stood up abruptly. "No!" Turning to Pito, she said, "We were brought here for a reason. We can't give up! Call the other parrots. Let's see if together we can get this giant to wake up and save our beloved island."

Realizing the gravity of the situation, Pito decided it was time to use the most powerful of all parrot calls—the Puerto Rican Parrot Unity Call. When other parrots heard this call, they would know their help was needed *pronto*—as in *life or death, pronto*! Pito stretched out his wings and took flight to the sky with purposeful impetus. Flying in circles, he squawked so loudly it seemed the entire island could hear his cry.

Suddenly, dozens and dozens of parrots swarmed the area, most landing on the ground since the trees at the top of the mountain were sparse. "What's the emergency?" a parrot cried out.

But when the parrots realized Pito had called them to the Sleeping Giant, they were furious.

"Pito, you know the law of the parrots. Using the Puerto Rican Parrot Unity Call is forbidden unless it's a matter of life and death! I can't believe you called us to wake a fake giant."

"But it *is* a matter of life and death, my brothers and sisters. The time has arrived for us to unite like never before to save our beloved rainforest—to save our enchanted island. We need your help waking the Sleeping Giant!"

"Wait!" Magia screamed at the top of her little coquí voice. "We have the magic! We saw it when I read the stone, and my little brother used the magic to swim in the river! We have it, and we only need to use it!"

The parrots gathered around like football players in a huddle. After some murmuring, one of the parrots said, "Okay, we'll try. But most of us still think this is a lost cause."

Magia said, "Lost causes are the best ones to fight for."

"This is not the time for doubt or fear!" Pito said. "This is the time for hope! We need you! Please."

Despite the questions, doubts, and uncertainty, they positioned themselves strategically. They created a deafening wall of noise loud enough to wake up the entire island at once.

Magia used her booming voice to join in, Guanito wailed on the strings of his cuatro, and Mateo oinked as loudly and obnoxiously as he could muster. All squawked, oinked, strummed, and croaked as if their life depended on it—all except one.

CHAPTER 12

Guanito noticed Luca, frozen still, from a distance, drowning in the sound wave without contributing. Guanito rushed over to him.

"Mijo, are you okay? Don't you want to help?"

But Luca did not respond. Something in him had shut down. His wings trembled. Guanito could see he was overcome with sadness. "I miss my Papi!" Luca said. He stumbled over his words with deep emotion. "I wish he were here. He'd know how to wake up the giant!"

Guanito put his tiny arms around him as they watched the parrots, Magia, and Mateo, yelling in an improvised chorus.

Suddenly, with everyone screeching as loud as they could, something unthinkable happened before their eyes.

The mountain started lifting, breaking from the seams of the earth. They all heard a loud crackling sound as the giant figure loosened itself from the soil. As he detached, the dirt fell from his massive body in sheets. Dry leaves were entangled in the giant's long dark hair. His face was covered in moss and dry flowers.

Everyone was transfixed by this miraculous moment. The giant slowly opened his mouth, and a thunderous sound spilled forward from the corners of his lips. The sound echoed across the rainforest and Puerto Rico, awakening all its inhabitants and creatures.

As he continued lifting from the earth's corners, it became clearer that he was a gigantic giant, but not just any giant. He was indeed a human Taino giant. Hiding behind a fallen log directly in front of the giant's mouth, the children, Guanito, and the parrots looked away in terror, imagining being swallowed by the giant's abysmal yawn.

The birds flew up and out of reach, leaving the trio and Guanito on the quaking ground.

"We're going to die!" Mateo screamed.

The children and Guanito held each other tightly, bouncing across the moving earth beneath them. The tight grip of the children's hug was quickly broken as Yukahú reached down and gently picked them up. The four found themselves sitting in the palm of his hand, gazing into Yukahú's eyes.

"*Hola*, my friends! Why do you look so shocked? Did you *not* mean to wake me?"

Hola: Hello

Pito flew up and landed beside the foursome. "Yukahú, I knew you were real!"

Yukahú laughed, and the ground trembled. Everyone screamed.

Yukahú smiled. "I'm sorry about that. I didn't mean to scare you!"

Pito gave out a call that let the parrots know that it was safe to return, and with a rush of wings they found places to perch on the mountainside and all over Yukahú's body. There were parrots on his shoulders, his arms, his hands, and even his head.

"Yes, I am real. I am Yukahú, also known as the Sleeping Giant. I am the creator and the protector of this rainforest you call home." He had kindness in his voice—the type that evoked comfort and confidence in Pito, Guanito, and the children. Maybe not so much in Luca, although he was curious about this giant Taino. Getting home felt closer than ever.

Magia was the first to speak up. "Greetings, Yukahú. We have come to you hoping that you could help us save the rainforest from the hurricane's devastation." She spoke quickly as if the giant might fall back asleep before she was able to get her words out.

"And help us return home," Luca said, gulping.

Everybody's eyes were fixed on Yukahú as they waited for his response. "Where is home, Señor Gallo?" Yukahú asked.

Magia answered the giant. "Well, if home is where the heart is, then home would be Puerto Rico."

Luca pushed her to the side. "But, we live in Buffalo now, and that's where we need to return. We were brought here by the magic."

He squinted his eyes, taking in their requests. "Oh, amigos, I cannot help. I do not have the answer to your question. I do not control the magic." Yukahú was visibly moved to sadness as he realized how difficult this information would be for them to hear.

No longer able to contain his feelings, Luca crowed with disbelief and judgement. "Whaaaaaat! Whaaaaaaat! Whaaaaaaat! Whaaaaaat! Whaaaaaaat! What do you mean you cannot help? You're going to tell me that we were magically transported to the rainforest through a closet, transformed into a rooster, a pig and a coquí, and you cannot help us save the rainforest or go back home?"

Magia tried to place a hand on Luca, but he kept pacing back and forth. She had never seen him so upset. He stomped in circles. His wings seemed to be keeping tempo with his fury as he shouted. "What kind of a protector are you? How can you let such horrible things happen to the ones you're supposed to take care of? You don't even know what it's like to lose something! You can't do anything!"

Exhausted from his rage, Luca collapsed into a feathery pile in the giant's hand.

Magia and Mateo could see what had been coming for a long time: their brother was finally breaking down. Rather than storming off and hiding, he said exactly how he felt, and they felt the same way.

Pito's voice trembled as he asked, "Are you saying there is no hope?" He looked into the giant's eye.

"You are our last hope," Magia said.

Mateo whispered, "Our last hope."

CHAPTER 13

"I'm so sorry, my children." Yukahú placed the children on the ground and knelt to be closer to them and the small group of animals clustered at his feet, though his face was still a couple of stories above them. "I know what this forest has gone through. I ache when she aches. I hurt when she hurts."

"Then why don't you fix it all?" Mateo asked. "We need you to give us hope."

Yukahú smiled a gentle, sad smile. "I cannot give you hope because it's not mine to give." A chilling silence permeated the air hovering over the rainforest with deep sadness and hopelessness.

"This forest has been around for longer than you can imagine—generations upon generations of humans and animals. I know how infuriating it is that sometimes the devastation comes fast, and healing may come slow. But the forest was created in the same manner. She will make it. Remember, she has survived countless hurricanes before, and she will grow back again. The hardest part is learning to have patience and grace between the hurricane and the healing. It is not something I enjoy in the slightest. But it is also not something I can or will snap my fingers and fix. There is resilience in this soil. You don't have to trust me, but it will be easier for you if you do."

"What are we supposed to do with this? What are we supposed to do in the meantime?" Magia croaked.

The mournful silence was suffocating, and not one of them moved. Luca had stopped crying, out of breath.

Always one to resort to music to express his deepest emotions, Guanito began strumming a song that carried the likes of a crying heart in each chord. As he strummed, the music became louder. Before long, the melody wafted through the hot air like a cool breeze.

The children looked at each other. Recognizing the melody brought a familiar feeling that reminded them of home.

Luca looked away. Guanito's strumming began stirring within him a sadness that he didn't quite understand.

"Please stop strumming," he whispered inside of his beak. But Guanito ignored him.

"Please stop strumming that song on the cuatro," he whispered once again. Guanito kept strumming.

Suddenly, Luca felt an energy rise deep in his chest. It was a song he had sung long ago with Papi—a song enveloped by the love between a father and son. It went like this:

Le lo le lo
Le lo le lo
Le lo le lo
Le lo lai

All eyes were on Luca, a green glow now surrounding him. Magia and Mateo looked on in disbelief, shocked by Luca and his loud crowing song. It was *the* Le Lo Lai song Papi used to play on his cuatro and sing to them when they were little. A melody they could barely remember but that Luca had obviously never forgotten. Luca had found his magic.

Luca couldn't stop himself. He didn't want to stop himself. All the notes returned fresh from a well of love in his memory. Then just as the rivers pour into the ocean, Luca poured out all the feelings he'd been bottling up for so long. *I really miss you, Papi. Anytime I was discouraged, you played your cuatro and sang the Le Lo Lai song until I fell asleep.*

Le lo le lo
Le lo le lo
Le lo le lo
Le lo lai
Le lo le lo
Le lo le lo
Le lo le lo
Le lo lai

Luca continued to sing, repeating the chorus over and over again, moving closer to hope with each note. "I didn't know Luca could sing so beautifully," Magia whispered to Mateo.

"I didn't know either," Mateo said.

One by one, the parrots joined in. An angelic choir grew as each parrot took up the song. The music of hope filled the rainforest's empty spaces, reverberating throughout each devastated corner of Puerto Rico. Pito, Magia, and Mateo began singing. Finally, even the Sleeping Giant sang, accompanied by Guanito and his cuatro.

The hope of the Le Lo Lai song—the ancestral words of celebration—strung together with the sound of the cuatro and the parrots' voices. Together, they created an invitation for restoration for Puerto Rico. The parrots knew they needed to spread this melody to everyone on the island. They flew away, carrying this song of hope to all the trees in the forest, and many landed on the branches of the Flamboyan. She lifted her sad branches into the air for the first time, breathing in the possibility of a new beginning.

More birds took up the song, as did the animals on the ground. The special song filled the air and wafted into the windows of the people holding their heads in their hands. Once the people started to sing, everything changed. They came out into their yards and hugged each other. Food was prepared and shared in the streets while hammers swung and rebuilding began.

A magical glowing light swept the island, with every note and chord. The rainforest's friends chimed in with their voices. The island's people let out the sorrowful sigh that had been stored deep within their souls, rooted in pain and loss. Collectively, they breathed in the hope of the Le Lo Lai song.

From their perch on the mountaintop, they could see Flamboyan far in the distance. The parrots landed on her broken branches and sang with such love and kindness. When the tree lifted her branches, bright red flowers burst forth simultaneously as green foliage covered vacant spaces. She held her head high with Puerto Rican pride, *orgullo*, touching the sky. The roots of her trunk pressed deeper into the earth, finding moist soil to drink further underground. Nature's canopy began spreading back over the rainforest, protecting the trees from the sweltering sun. Parrots had a place to build their nests. All rainforest creatures knew they would be safe again.

orgullo:
pride

Yukahú bowed reverently enjoying the unfolding beauty of this moment. He looked down at the children and said, "You see, the forest didn't need to be fixed. It was created to fix itself. And you never needed me to give you hope. It was already inside of you, and always will be. Sometimes sadness and loss can make us forget who we are and where we come from.

Luca said, "We are from Puerto Rico."

"Yes, you are," nodded the giant. He smiled turning his attention back to the majestic blend of harmonies. "And so are they." He waved his arm across the landscape below them. As each village took up the song, it became louder and fuller. "Oh, how sweet is the sound of the people singing together. Today they remember that they are strong and resilient. It's their love for each other and for their island that makes Puerto Rico such a magical place. And they've rediscovered that the magic of our island can always be found in its music."

Magia let out a huge sigh. "They're ready now, aren't they, Yukahu?"

The Sleeping Giant smiled, "Yes, Magia. They are ready. It's time to rebuild."

CHAPTER 14

The sun set on the island, still abuzz with activity, laughter and the sounds of people making plans for the next day's activities. Yukahú, Pito, Guanito, and the children sat watching the lights in the houses go on, one by one.

"What a splendid moment," Guanito said softly as everybody looked in his direction.

"I forgot you were here," Mateo said innocently.

"I forgot I was here too," Guanito said with a chuckle. "This is why I play the cuatro. So, if you don't see me, at least you can hear me." Everybody laughed. Their joy was as palpable as the rainforest's restored warmth, sun, and fresh tropical breeze.

As the stars came up, Yukahú turned to the group with wide, childlike eyes. "Do you see those four stars?" He pointed his giant finger toward the heavens as he questioned his newfound friends. The trio, Pito, and Guanito shifted their eyes to the sky and nodded yes with curiosity. "Do you know that I placed those four stars in the sky?"

"Actually, I remember learning about the four stars during Hispanic Heritage Month when Ms. Rivera had a guest speaker come to our school to speak about Taino History," Magia said. She proudly impressed even herself that she knew exactly what Yukahú was referring to.

"*Muy bien*, Magia," Yukahú smiled. Magia puffed out her tiny coquí chest like a brown birthday balloon.

muy bien: very good

"Sweet!" Mateo added with a proud smile.

"Luca, amigo, are you okay?" Pito asked.

Luca broke his silence with the question he'd been holding. "Yukahú, if you were able to place those stars in the sky, you most definitely are capable of placing us back in Buffalo, right?"

"Not quite. You see, the rainforest called you here for two reasons. The first is to use your magic to help Puerto Rico."

"Which we did," Luca said, surprised by that realization.

"What's the second reason?" Magia asked.

"The magic always likes to teach you something—give you something you can take back with you. The lesson will come as surely as the stones are held in the sky without knowing how, when, or why."

"Respectfully, the only thing I want to learn is how to go back home," Luca said.

Yukahú looked lost in thought for a moment. Then he turned to Mateo. "Mateo, what is in your pocket?"

Mateo looked stunned. "How do you know?" Reaching inside his blue overalls with his cloven piggy toes, Mateo pulled out something tiny and blue.

Magia hopped over and was astonished by the stone before her eyes. She knew this was not just any blue stone. This was *the* stone. The stone native to Puerto Rico. The *Larimar* stone, also known as the love stone. Her Papi had given her Mami a Larimar necklace on their tenth wedding anniversary. Sometimes Magia would wear it when she wanted to feel her Papi close to her heart.

Larimar: a rare, blue gemstone found only in this region, often used in jewelry

Luca, too, recognized this stone, inhaling sharply. He cried out, "When did you get this?"

"I found it when we picked up stones to throw at Yukahú. It was so pretty. I didn't want to throw it." He felt guilty. "It reminded me of Papi's bright eyes." Mateo had inherited his Papi's eye color. "So I kept it. I wanted to take it back home to show Mami."

Magia smiled and hugged her brother. "I would have done the same thing."

Luca asked, "Is it because Mateo stole that stone that we can't go home?"

Mateo protested. "I didn't *steal* it. I just didn't throw it."

Yukahú picked up the stone and held it in his large palm. "The four stars that are now in the sky were once stones just like this one."

"Stones!" Mateo exclaimed in awe of the giant and his powers.

"Yes, the stones are now in the sky, lighting the way and guiding us at night."

Yukahú looked around for Luca. "Come, my friend Luca. Stand next to me," he said rather assertively. Luca thought it would be prudent to listen to the Sleeping Giant, especially after losing his temper a few times, which he felt bad about. He walked over to Yukahú as everybody watched and waited, wondering why he had been called over. He stood next to the giant's ginormous mossy toe.

"Now, pay close attention to what I'm going to say." Yukahú held the Larimar stone up high and proceeded to string words together that would be forever etched in his memory and sealed in his heart. These are the words he would never forget:

"Up in the sky four stones
A fifth stone soon to be known
A bright star in the sky
As bright and blue as Papi's eyes
A forever reminder of love kept alive."

Suddenly the Larimar stone magically lifted from the giant's palm as four stars danced and twirled in the sky. Clapping and bravos could be heard from above, marking the trajectory of the stones with celebration and awe. Heaven's stars shifted, creating space for its brand-new companion, now shining brightly from afar.

"You can't make this stuff up," Guanito exclaimed as he strummed his cuatro, enthralled by this magical moment. Pito looked on, grateful to have been a witness. Magia and Mateo were gazing at the newly placed star in Papi's honor when they heard a loud crow coming from Luca's direction.

CHAPTER 15

"Luca, are you okay?" asked Mateo.

"This is it! This is what the magic wants us to take back with us. The lesson!" Everybody looked at Luca, waiting for him to share.

"Oh! This is my favorite part," said Yukahú. "It's when everything comes together for our traveling companions!" Yukahú marked his words with anxious expectancy. He looked at Luca with compassion and said, "Go on, my friend."

"I don't have to forget about my Papi, right? Even though when I think about him, I feel really sad inside here." He pointed at his white feathery chest. "I can think about him and remember him because when I do, I remember how much he loves me, and how much I love him. Right? Is that it?" Luca asked timidly with his eyes lowered, afraid that he might be wrong but hopeful that he might be right.

"Yes! Indeed!" Yukahú proclaimed joyously. "And now, there will always be a blue star in the sky to remind you of your Papi's love—forever!" Yukahú smiled. For once, Magia had nothing to add, and she smiled in agreement with Luca—a rare but welcomed occurrence. She knew how much Luca needed this moment.

"My man!" Mateo fist pumped in the air. "Big brother Luca! You are supah dupah!" He clapped for Luca as he laughed. His laugh produced snorting sounds that he couldn't control, making him laugh and snort even harder.

Suddenly, the Le Lo Lai song that had drawn them to the closet wafted through the air. Everyone stopped to listen. The song grew louder.

"Is that…?" Mateo asked.

"I think so," responded Magia.

A crackling sound was heard coming from beneath the bed of flowers that covered the rainforest's floor. Leaves jumped joyously as they swirled in the air. Suddenly, the grass parted, giving way to an open space. A glowing light surrounded the children, staging what was shaping up to be the grand finale to Magia's story. There it was! The magical closet door!

Scan this code to listen to the Magical Closet song.

The trio stood silently, looking at each other and at their new friends. How odd to feel gladness and sadness at the same time. Although they were happy the door back home had finally reappeared, they were sad about leaving Guanito, Pito, and Yukahú. The siblings looked at each other with deep love, and in silent agreement, they marched forward toward the door. Stopping suddenly, Luca looked back to wave goodbye. He said, "Call us when you need us again." Yukahú nodded in their direction, motioning with his giant hands for them to continue their journey back home.

A few steps later, Luca hit his head on a closet pole. He rubbed his head and looked down at his human feet! The first thing to come into focus was a white, navy, and gold jersey, number twenty-one. "Roberto Clemente!" Luca shrieked, snatching up the filthy jersey and hugging it tightly.

He looked over at Magia and Mateo, gently tugging his sister's braids and poking his brother's arm. The trio hugged, laughed, and celebrated. They were back home!

Magia stopped in her tracks and turned to her brothers. "We promise to keep this a secret. Right?"

Mateo agreed. "No one would believe us anyway."

Luca agreed. "They would say we were nuts."

Mateo laughed. "I think they might say that anyway." They all giggled.

Magia and Mateo treaded forward through the bedroom, talking and laughing.

Tía Clara's footsteps were approaching in the hallway. She entered carrying a plate of pizza pastelillos. Apparently, on this side of the door, hardly any time had passed since Mami left. Magia, Luca, and Mateo shouted with delight at the sight of the long-awaited snack.

"Yes! My favorite! Oh yeah! Oh yeah!" Mateo voiced his excitement with song and dance as he jumped on his bed.

"Que rico—delicious!" Magia said as she bit into the warm, flaky snack. Luca said nothing because his mouth was already full of food.

que rico:
how delicious

Later that night, when everyone in the house was asleep, Luca quietly snuck out of bed and entered the closet one more time. The back of the closet looked the same as it always did. There was nothing magical about it at all.

Was it really true? Did he and his brother and sister actually travel to Puerto Rico through this closet? Did Papi have magic that was passed down to them? It seemed like a dream rather than something that could be real.

He was about to close the door when he saw something on the floor—something soft, silky, green, red, and blue. He looked closer, reached down, and picked up a feather. It looked exactly like a feather from a Puerto Rican Parrot! He picked it up and it glowed. A magical gift from Pito, no doubt. *It really did happen.* He smiled as he walked toward the blue chest next to his bed.

Reaching deep inside the top drawer, he pulled out a book he had hidden in the chest after Papi died. Papi had bought him a book about firefighters for his birthday but wasn't able to give it to him before he passed. It had been too painful for Luca to look at it, so he'd never opened it before.

Now, Luca knew it was time to open the book. He took a deep breath for courage. As he turned the pages, tears filled his eyes and rolled down his cheeks. Every image was a reminder of Papi, of how much he missed and loved him. He placed the feather between the crisp pages. Fresh on his mind were the echoing sounds of El Yunque and the Le Lo Lai.

Moving through the dark to the window, he looked up into the night sky. It took a few moments to locate the five-star constellation, but finally he found it. There was the fifth star—Papi's star.

He was sure it would be shining in the sky exactly where Yukahú placed it. He smiled as he whispered to himself, "I'll remember to look for the star every night because remembering keeps the love alive."

Remembering keeps the love alive.

Acknowledgments

The journey of bringing this book to life has been one of the most magical—and mysterious—I have ever encountered. Just as we watch our children grow, this story has continuously become more beautiful and authentic at each stage. Key people have shaped this book into what it was meant to be, and equally, others have shaped me into the person I needed to be to tell the story. It is my honor to acknowledge those people here.

I want to start by thanking my team at Berry Powell Press. When I first read Carmen Renee Berry's book, *When Helping You is Hurting Me*, over twenty-five years ago, I could never have imagined that one day she would be publishing *my* book! Both Carmen and Abigail Dengler have encapsulated the very definition of support, creativity, and vision. A special bond is forged between those who have weathered the creative process together. Also, from the Berry Powell team, I want to thank Valeri Mills Barnes, Marianne Croonquist, Carolyn Rafferty, and Kathleen Taylor for your invaluable creative input and dedication. Adriana Penberthy provided insight that strengthened the message, and Roy Carlisle shared his wisdom in positioning the book and making Luca's journey realistic. Brianna Manocchio made me a website that bursts with joy and authenticity.

For the gorgeous illustrations and design, it's my joy to thank Carlos Torres and Kay McConnaughey. Carlos, your images perfectly capture my love for Puerto Rico. I can't wait for fellow *boricuas* to see their homeland on these pages. Those who have never seen it will witness its magic through your pencil. Kay, thank you for your dedication and care in ensuring the design pops off the shelf and into young readers' hands.

For those who don't know, The Magical Closet was first born as a ten-minute musical performed with Raíces Theatre Company. Raíces family, ensemble members, and original cast, you gave this story its first wings to soar. Wilmer Olivencia, thank you for offering a space to tell this story. Smirna Mercedes, you gave me a quiet space to write when I most needed it. Rafi Mencía, you captured this story's magic through the lens of your camera. Michele Agosto, your narration is magical. Francisco Vaquero, thank you for your willingness to provide a space for rehearsals. Rafael Pérez, Keven Doyle, and Sara Rodríguez, you brought the original music to life—and Sara, you knew it would become a book long before I did. You held that vision for me until I could reach it.

Though the story evolved into a book, it could never fully be captured without music. For that reason, I am so grateful to my son, Alejandro Gabriel Gómez, for capturing my vision in song. Thank you, Manny Pérez, for saying yes to the children. Manolo Ramos, I'm in awe of your talent, humble heart, and willingness to journey with me. Lucía Ramos, you sing like an angel, and I believe you are one. Thank you, Adrián Guadalupe, for embracing my musical and saying yes to every new venture. Thank you, Santiago Hercé LoConti Alcocer, for being my little bestie, your sweet voice, and your willingness to sing for Tía Depi. Luis Manuel Santiago and Steven Guasch, you have been my Miguel Meléndez Muñoz brothers and have believed in me since the eighth grade. Lastly, thank you to Robin Lazzara for capturing my vision in the promo video with such joy.

I am honored by all who believed in me enough to read the book and give endorsements and reviews before it was published, including Kyle LoConti, Kate LoConti Alcocer, Matthew Tice, Victoria Pérez, John Anderson, Jennifer Anderson, Roberta Farkas-Huezo, Ingrid Córdova, Dr. Janyne McConnaughey, Abigail Grainge, and Michael Cline.

I am speechless when I think of those whose generosity made this adventure possible: Maggiolo-Pérez family, Eva and Rafael Pérez, Francisco and Renee Vaquero, Emilia Rodríguez-Tete, Francisco Guzman II, Julio Montalvo Valentín, Steven Guasch, Hispanic Heritage Council of WNY, Luis Manuel Santiago, Jeanette Torres, Julio García, Dr. Raúl Vázquez, and everyone who donated through Kickstarter.

My family, you are my life. Abuelo Jorge Rodríguez y Familia, you instilled in me my love of music. Mami and Mami (Elena), you gifted me with my love of children. Jeanie, you are my trusty cheerleader. Thank you, Victoria, my Seastar, for never wavering. Thank you, Lito, Oscar, Vicky, and Victor for a lifetime of memories. Alejandro, Ricardo, and Amara, thank you for giving me purpose. Bebo and Keyla, thank you for your love of my vision and for believing in me. And Rolando, my words fall short. Thank you for your unconditional love, for steering my ship through the storms, and for being the love of my life. You are my everything.

To Anita and Mariel, remembering keeps the love alive, and I love you every day.

Lastly, thank you to everyone who leaned in, listened, and loved me during this journey. For wisdom, grace, and serendipitous encounters, I thank The Divine.

About the Author

Born in Buffalo, NY, María Pérez-Gómez moved to Puerto Rico when she was eleven after the tragic loss of her baby brother. While she has lived in Buffalo for most of her adult life, María is "as *boricua* as a *coquí*." She's as profoundly Puerto Rican as the little frog whose constant song has made it emblematic of the island itself. Her greatest goal as an artist is to craft stories in which other Latino(é) children can see themselves and help children of all backgrounds develop resilience.

In addition to being an author, María has a long history as a playwright, performer, and vocalist. She is Managing Director for Raíces Theatre Company, the only Latino(é) theatre company in western New York. She has written several plays and musicals for Raíces, including the ten-minute musical *The Magical Closet*, from which the book developed. Alongside her husband and children, María has performed the original play of *The Magical Closet* for dozens of audiences across the country. She also recently co-wrote and directed the play *ISLEÑA* alongside her sister.

A lover of various mediums, María has partnered with local artists Sara Rodríguez, Alejandro Gómez, and renowned Puerto Rican composer, singer, and producer Manolo Ramos, for the music that accompanies this adventure.

When María isn't creating, writing, or composing, she works as the Assistant Director at Vive, a shelter for asylum seekers. One of María's greatest joys is being a mother to her three biological and two "bonus" children—and being married to the love of her life.

For more information go to www.themagicalclosetmyseries.com

About the Illustrator

Carlos Torres is an award-winning illustrator whose work has appeared in such publications as *Time*, *Sports Illustrated*, *Barron's*, *National Review*, *Los Angeles Times*, and *Chicago Tribune*. Over the years, his clients have included Pepsi, American Airlines, Macy's, DuPont, Time Warner, and Scholastic.

Known for his editorial caricatures, one of Torres's works, "Chairman Nixon," was part of a national traveling exhibition hosted by the New York City-based Society of Illustrators.

More recently, his personal works have included a series of carousel horse images inspired by the historic Herschell Carrousel Museum located in North Tonawanda, New York, where he lives.

Born and raised in New York City, Torres has now been a North Tonawanda resident for nearly thirty years with his wife Claudia and their three boys.

When not working on a deadline, Torres also enjoys teaching art to students ranging from preschoolers at an early childhood center to private lessons for adults at his studio.

For more information go to www.torresart.com

A Note from the Publisher

We at Berry Powell Press are delighted to publish María Pérez-Gómez's book, *The Magical Closet Mystery: A Puerto Rican Adventure*. This book embodies our values and fulfills the reason BPP exists. First, the story comes from María's personal experience dealing with loss and making the difficult transition of moving from Puerto Rico to the State of New York.

Second, the story's characters experience their journey of healing and hope, learning skills based on solid psychological principles. The book has depth and nuance that allows for increasing emotional intelligence for young and adult readers alike.

Third, the book is written in such a way as to expand a child's understanding of the Spanish language, along with celebrating the cultural diversity of Puerto Rico. Elements included are the folklore of the indigenous Taino people, the historical ethnic composition of its people, the threat of potential extinction of the Puerto Rican parrot, the increasing devastation brought on by climate change, and the landmarks and delights of this small but beautiful island.

The Berry Powell Press staff is committed to cultivating authors and their life-changing messages through building a collaborative creative community of authors and publishing professionals. Do you have a book rumbling around inside of you that needs to be written and released? Please visit our website at www.berrypowellpress.com. Contact us, and we can explore together if we might be a fit.

Berry Powell Press is a hybrid publishing house that publishes authors with transformational perspectives on timely personal and societal challenges. We provide our authors with in-depth mentorship & collaborative assistance to create life-changing books. Additionally, we assist them in building book-based businesses that can impact the largest audience possible. We publish fiction and non-fiction for adults and children.

Made in the USA
Las Vegas, NV
12 December 2024